POWER HITTER
Christine A. Forsyth

James Lorimer & Company Ltd., Publishers
Toronto

James Lorimer & Company Ltd., Publishers acknowledges the support of the Ontario Arts Council. We acknowledge the financial support of the Government of Canada through the Canada Book Fund for our publishing activities. We acknowledge the support of the Canada Council for the Arts which last year invested $24.3 million in writing and publishing throughout Canada. We acknowledge the Government of Ontario through the Ontario Media Development Corporation's Ontario Book Initiative.

Cover image: Tate Nations

Library and Archives Canada Cataloguing in Publication

Forsyth, C. A. (Christine A.), author
    Power hitter / Christine A. Forsyth.

(Sports stories)
First published in 2001.
Issued in print and electronic formats.
ISBN 978-1-4594-0590-5 (pbk.).—ISBN 978-1-4594-0592-9 (epub)

    I. Title. II. Series: Sports stories (Toronto, Ont.)

PS8561.O6966P68 2014   jC813'.54   C2013-906569-5
C2013-906570-9

James Lorimer & Company Ltd.,
Publishers
317 Adelaide Street West, Suite 1002
Toronto, ON, Canada
M5V 1P9
www.lorimer.ca

Distributed in the United States by:
Orca Book Publishers
P.O. Box 468
Custer, WA USA
98240-0468

Printed and bound in Canada.
Manufactured by Webcom in Toronto, Ontario in March 2014.
Job #411700

For Griffin and Connor and their friends.

CONTENTS

1 SKY HIGH

It was my first time in an airplane and I thought I knew what to expect. But when we took off, I wasn't prepared for the way the plane tilted up, pushing me back into my seat. The old guy next to me said it was just like sitting in your living room easy chair. Yeah, except the floor was pointed toward the sky and there was all this weird clanking and whirring under my feet. Finally, the plane broke through the clouds and the sunlight on the wing almost blinded me.

Somewhere down there, miles behind us, was Burlington, Ontario, my house, and my mom. She was probably at home busy getting ready to go into the hospital in a couple of days. Probably worried. She'd been worried ever since my dad left. That was two years ago, when I was eleven. We hadn't seen him since then, although he called every month from Florida, where he went to work. On the phone, he told me all about Orlando and the theme parks where we'd go on rides every day, once Mom and I moved there to be with him. I didn't know when that was going to be, because I gave up asking.

Well, I finally got to go on a big ride, but I wasn't headed for Orlando — just Winnipeg. I had a card in my jeans' pocket. On one side it had my name, Connor Wells, with my address and phone number in Burlington. On the other side was the name and address of a family of distant relatives — Jane Campbell, my mom's second cousin, her husband, Andrew, and their two kids, Griffin, who was twelve, and Claire, who was nine. I was going to spend my entire summer vacation with relatives I'd never met, while my mother went into the hospital for something too serious to even tell me about.

The plane hit a bump in the sky and some of my pop splashed out of the cup onto the old guy next to me. "Sorry," I said, even though it wasn't my fault.

"Don't worry, son," he replied, wiping his jacket with a big handkerchief. "That was just a little turbulence. It happens all the time. Absolutely nothing to worry about."

"I'm not worried," I told him. At least, not much. I figured that since there was nothing to run into up there we must have been pretty safe.

"Is your family in Winnipeg, son?"

How come old guys always call you "son," I wondered? Like my grandpa does. My dad never called me "son." He always called me "kid," or "pal," or even "dude" sometimes. "What?" I said, when I realized the old guy was staring at me.

"Do you have family in Winnipeg?" he repeated.

"No," I replied. "Well, sort of. There are these people that my mother knows, actually they're cousins but not like close cousins." I was beginning to sound like an idiot.

"Going to stay with them, are you?" he asked.

"Yeah," I said. "They've got kids. The boy is around my age."

He asked me how old I was — thirteen — and then he said I was pretty big for my age. It was true. My mom says I grow like a weed because I went from five foot nothing to five foot five in just over a year. I'm pretty solid too, like my dad. And I eat a lot.

When the pilot announced that we were making our descent, we broke through the clouds and Winnipeg appeared below us. The old guy leaned over me to point out the window.

"That's the Red River down there. That one flooded a few years back. It joins up with the Assiniboine at a place called The Forks. You should ask your cousins to take you there. You'll like it." The man continued to point out things as the plane descended. I hardly noticed the sounds the engines made because I was fascinated by the rivers. We lived near Lake Ontario, and sometimes Mom and I would go to a park by the water or to the public beach for picnics and swimming. The lake was okay, but I liked rivers way better. You can go places on rivers.

Once, I spent a week at my friend's cottage on a river in Muskoka. It was awesome. We paddled a canoe up and down the river, pulling ashore to explore whenever we saw something interesting. My friend's dad took us through some locks in his powerboat. That was totally amazing. We motored in through these big gates and when the gates closed behind us, the water inside was let out. Slowly, the water level dropped and the boat rode lower and lower in the lock. It was so cool, sinking down between the dark, wet walls. Finally, the water stopped flowing out and the doors at the other end opened for us to leave. Try that on Lake Ontario!

I didn't have time to ask the man if there were locks on the rivers in Winnipeg. As soon as the plane was on the ground, everybody popped out of their seats, getting ready to leave.

Out in the terminal I was supposed to stay near the exit and wait for someone to "recognize" me. My mom had texted a picture of me to her cousin. I wasn't sure which side of the door to stand at, so I just stood in the middle. People kept hitting me with their bags as they crashed around.

Out of nowhere, a woman with long brown hair and really cool black glasses, with red, white, and yellow polka dots on them, appeared in front in me. "Connor! Welcome to Winnipeg!" she exclaimed, loudly. People turned to look at us and I felt my face heat up. She was holding up her cell phone and I could see my picture on it. She announced, "I brought this just in case there was more than one tall, thirteen-year-old boy with blond, curly hair."

My face got redder while I stood there, mute. "I'm Jane," she said, smiling widely, "and this is Claire." I looked at the kid beside Jane and mumbled something.

"Hi, Connor," Claire said, grinning. She also had dark brown hair, like her mother, but hers was cut short and kind of stuck out all over her head. When she smiled, her brown eyes closed almost completely. If I were her, I wouldn't want to walk and smile at the same time. It could be dangerous.

We stood around the baggage carousel waiting for my dad's old hockey bag to appear. It was the last one down and I was getting nervous thinking that they'd lost it or something. My bag was the only one in the whole airport that wasn't on wheels so Jane got a cart and we dumped the bag onto it and rolled out to the parking lot.

After my gear was stowed in the back of their green minivan, Jane invited me to sit up front so I could have a better view of the city. It didn't look a lot different than where I came from.

"This is Main Street, Connor," Jane said. "The windiest intersection in North America is behind us, downtown at Portage and Main." I guessed Jane had never driven over the Skyway Bridge, in Burlington, when the wind blew down the lake.

"Where's the river?" I asked.

"The Red River is over to your right. You can't see it from here, but our house is quite close to it."

Yes! I began imagining how I would spend my summer hanging out by the river, canoeing, or maybe rafting. A raft would be very cool. I could fish and swim. Things were looking up in Winnipeg, I thought.

"We're here," Jane said, pulling into a parking lot. I was confused. There were tons of people wandering around a big park with trees and tennis courts. Maybe we were going camping. I got out of the van and went around the back to get my bag out, but Jane and Claire took off. Claire turned around and yelled, "Come on. They've already started."

I had no idea who "they" were or what they'd "started" but I followed Jane and Claire anyway. Beyond the trees was a baseball diamond and we climbed into the stands, zigging and zagging until we reached a dark-haired man sitting alone.

"Connor," Jane said, "this is my husband, Andrew." Andrew stood up, blocking out the sun, and a huge shadow fell over me. He was a really big guy, maybe even a foot taller than I was. He stuck out a giant hand, the size of a frisbee.

"Very pleased to meet you, Connor," he said. "Welcome to Winnipeg."

I shook his hand, feeling like I had climbed a beanstalk and met a giant.

"Sit here, Connor," he said, indicating the seat beside him. "Our team is the Spinners. They're the ones on the field, wearing the red and white jerseys." When Andrew finally sat down, the sun came out again. Claire sat beside me and Jane sat on the other side of Andrew.

"Do you play baseball, Connor?" Andrew asked.

"No, sir," I replied, looking down onto the field where kids my age appeared to be standing around doing nothing — which is exactly what I thought baseball was all about.

"That's our son, Griffin," Jane said, pointing to a half-sized Andrew clone standing in the middle of a big hump of dirt. The clone wound up and fired a ball at another kid standing with a bat on his shoulder, wearing a blue plastic hat. The kid in the plastic hat swatted at the ball, but the catcher ended up with it. Another guy, standing around behind the catcher, yelled something and the catcher threw the ball back to the clone. There, I thought, that's baseball. Time for a nap.

No such luck. Andrew, after yelling something encouraging to Griffin, explained that it was his first time as the starting pitcher. Andrew had been practising with him to improve his "control" and the team had "high hopes" for Griffin to become their star pitcher for the season. Sheesh! You'd have thought the kid was pitching for the Blue Jays in the World Series or something, the way those people were talking.

Hey, it's not like I'd never seen a baseball game. I'd watched a few on TV, with my dad. Once, we were supposed to go to Toronto to see the Jays, but my dad had to work late. After he left for Florida, I kind of lost interest.

Another kid in a plastic hat faced Griffin. He swung at the first pitch and lost his balance. Claire snickered beside me. While he waited for the batter to get into position, Griffin glanced up at us. The batter swung away at the next pitch, with the same result. Claire's snickering became a full out laugh. I was feeling a little sorry for the batter, especially when he fell over completely, missing the next pitch.

Claire shouted, "Smokin'!" as the inning ended. Griffin's team headed for the bench, while the other team took to the field. Before Griffin sat down, he looked up into the stands and waved at us. I felt stupid waving back to a total stranger, but I would have felt stupider not waving at all.

The first batter of the inning hit the first pitch, but I couldn't see where the ball went. I was looking all over the place. Finally, I noticed a lot of kids running in the outfield near the fence. One of them picked up the ball and lobbed it into the infield. When the dust settled, the batter was on second base and Griffin, who had been waiting his turn at bat, walked up to the plate.

"Hey," I said. "I thought the pitchers didn't hit."

Andrew chuckled and said, "We don't have designated hitters in Little League, Connor. Everybody has a turn at bat."

"Oh," was all I could think of to say. I was a little embarrassed but nobody noticed because the family's eyes were glued on Griffin swinging his bat around. Andrew was running the play-by-play in my ear. The pitcher hurled the ball and Griffin just stood there and let it go by. "Good eye, Griffin!" yelled Andrew. "Ball one," he added — for my sake, I'm sure.

When the pitcher got around to flinging the ball again, Griffin took an almighty swing and I starting looking madly into the field. Claire, tugging on my shirt said, "He whiffed it." I guessed that meant he had a bad eye, but nobody said anything about that, except Claire, who announced that it was now one ball and one strike.

Griffin started doing all kinds of weird things with his head, like a bobble-head toy. He shrugged his shoulders a few times, and tapped the ground with the bat and then tapped his shoes. By the time he got lined up to hit again I was thinking that the game might never end. But he connected with the next pitch and again I searched in vain for the ball. Once more, Claire pointed me in the right direction. The ball was rolling into the outfield between second and third bases. At least I knew my bases.

Griffin ran like mad around first and second. He hesitated for a moment at second, and by the time he'd headed for third, the ball was on its way back from the outfield. He dove for the bag and the Campbells were on their feet. The guy behind the catcher made some hand signals and they broke into a cheer. Claire leaned in and whispered, "that means 'safe.'" While all this was going on, the kid who had been on second waltzed home.

Claire was chanting something that sounded like "arby eye," which I thought must mean the same thing as "good eye." I stuck to clapping until I could get the lingo down.

The next guy at bat was a big kid, like me. I noticed that he got a huge round of applause from a bunch of people sitting behind us when he stepped up to the plate. The applause faded as he whiffed the first pitch. Then he whiffed the next one and the one after that. The people behind us sat down and so did he.

Meanwhile, old Griffin was rooted to the bag at third. My attention was starting to wander. Then, the next batter struck out. Griffin had been planted on third so long he looked like he needed watering.

A skinny little guy who wasn't much bigger than Claire was swinging a bat that was almost as tall as he was. I didn't hold out much hope for him. Besides, nobody got up and cheered like mad when he stepped up to the plate. Imagine my surprise when he smacked the first pitch and it rolled into the outfield behind the pitcher. I looked at Claire for some guidance on the appropriate response and then realized that I'd actually seen where the ball went. Claire was looking at home plate, where Griffin had just scored. This baseball stuff was exhausting. First I couldn't see where the ball went, then I could, and when I could, I missed a run.

I had always thought that watching baseball was, as my dad used to say, "like watching paint dry." But even if the action wasn't constant, like in hockey or soccer, there was still some suspense. I started asking questions, so by the end of the game I knew a lot more than I had when I'd arrived. Like "arby eye" is actually RBI — short for run batted in.

In the end, Griffin's team won by just one run, which made the family really happy. They chatted and waved to other families in the stands as we stood to leave. Andrew put his hand on my shoulder. "Come and meet Griffin."

2 THE RIVER

Griffin didn't waste any time waiting for us to find him. He came running up to us like we were home plate and he was about to score the winning run. "Hi, Connor," he said, sticking his hand out for me to shake.

"Um, hi," I mumbled, thinking that this family had a weird thing about shaking hands.

Griffin was smiling like a madman. The rest of the family just stood around watching us like we were on TV or something. I didn't know what to say, so I just said, "Nice game." I didn't think it was possible for Griffin to smile any bigger, but he did.

"Do you play baseball?" he asked, looking at me hopefully.

"Uh, no," I answered, truthfully. I could see that I'd disappointed him, because the smile melted off his face. Finally Jane broke the silence and started raving about what a great game Griffin had pitched. In seconds, Griffin's smile was back.

We all shuffled off to the parking lot where we split

up into two carloads. I went with Griffin and Andrew in Andrew's green truck. My bag went with Jane and Claire. It was only a short drive from the park to their house and Griffin kept pointing out the window to things that weren't there. I mean, he kept saying things like "the forest is over there" and "the tree house is behind that big house over there." I just nodded my head and said things like "great" and "cool" because he kept looking at me for a reaction.

I was sort of glad when we pulled into their driveway. At least I wouldn't have to keep nodding like a puppet, I thought, but I wasn't expecting the show and tell to carry on into Griffin's bedroom. He dragged me upstairs and showed me where to put my stuff. Griffin's room was a lot bigger than mine was at home. It had one of those bunk beds where the lower bunk is bigger than the top bunk. I guessed that I would get the smaller one, but Griffin told me to take the bottom bunk. I decided Griffin was okay.

He had his own laptop and his own cell phone, which was pretty cool. Mom and I shared an ancient PC that was way too slow for gaming. If I wanted to do anything interesting on a computer, I had to go to one of my friends' houses. And since Dad left, there's no way we could afford a cell phone for me.

Griffin's room was totally about baseball. Every wall was covered with posters of baseball players. Most of them were pitchers, which gave me the impression

I was in the middle of a bunch of guys aiming baseballs at my head. There were shelves with baseballs and trophies and one of those big squishy hands with the pointing finger that fans wave around at games like I've seen on TV.

The room was really neat and tidy, like a room in a movie or a magazine. I hoped that Griffin didn't like to keep it that way all the time because I wasn't famous for my neatness. Actually, according to my mom, I was famous for my messiness. She said it's a genetic disorder I inherited from my dad, but I think it's because I just had better things to do.

"Hi-speed?" I asked, itching to get my hands on the computer.

"Extreme," Griffin replied, saying the magic word. I was glad he didn't ask me what kind I had. In fact, he was heading out the door. Reluctantly, I followed him, looking back at the computer with envy.

"Come on," Griffin said, as he disappeared around a corner. "I'll show you the neighbourhood."

I followed the sound of his voice, down the stairs and into a small office where Jane was sitting at a silver laptop with a huge external monitor.

"I'm going to show Connor around, okay, Mom?" Griffin announced.

Jane looked up from the screen. "Sure, Griffin," she replied. "Just be back by five-thirty for dinner." She smiled at me before turning back to the computer.

"How many computers do you have in your house?" I asked Griffin.

He looked at me kind of funny, like it was a weird question. "Four," he said. I was jealous. Everybody had their computer. "Unless you count iPads," he added. "We all have to those too, even Dad." Okay, now I was totally jealous. We were outside by then and I really wanted to go back in and check out the iPad.

Griffin was motoring away from the house so I guessed I'd have to wait. "Hey Griffin," I said, "how far is the river?"

"Not far, I was going to take you there anyway."

We walked along his street past houses that were similar to Griffin's. Most of them had two storeys with garages on the right side. I noticed that every lawn was freshly cut. A lot of people were outside because it was a nice day. Griffin waved and said hello to everybody. Halfway down the street, we stopped and Griffin went up to a house with a wide verandah. I stayed on the sidewalk, eyeing a Dalmatian sitting beside the fire hydrant down the street. I liked dogs all right, but we'd never had one and I was usually wary of dogs just running around free.

Griffin came back with the big, stocky kid who I'd seen strike out in the baseball game. He was wearing his baseball cap backwards and a tuft of brown hair stuck straight up out of the opening in the cap. "Connor, this is Austin," he said to me. Turning to Austin he said,

"This is my cousin, Connor. The one I told you about."
I kind of liked being called "cousin." I don't have any
cousins at home.

"I saw you in the game," I said to Austin. He just
laughed and struck out down the street. As we ap-
proached the dog, it just sat there, staring into the emp-
ty street. "What's with the zombie dog?" I asked.

Griffin and Austin laughed. Griffin ran ahead and
grabbed the dog around the neck. "What the . . . ?" I
gaped as he swung the dog up like it was a baseball bat.
Then I laughed too. It was a fake dog attached to the
hydrant with a real leash. When we caught up with him
he explained. "A firefighter lives here."

"They have a real Dalmatian inside," Austin added.
"They dress this one up like Santa Claus at Christmas,
and like a bunny at Easter."

"Yeah, and at Halloween they leave treats out for
him." said Griffin. "All the little kids in the neighbourhood really like it."

After that, we walked through a park with a bright
red slide. Continuing beyond the big house that Griffin
had pointed out earlier, we passed a tree house built into
a big, old tree. We walked through a field of roughly cut
grass leading to a forest that reminded me of the forest at the edge of the back pasture at my grandparents'
farm, except that this forest ended at the river.

Tons of people were hanging around that day, especially on a dock that jutted out into the river. Some

people were fishing, while others were just standing around looking at the water.

I went immediately out to the end of the dock, with Griffin and Austin following. "Are there fish?" I asked.

"Yeah," Griffin replied. "We can't keep them, though. We just throw them back because you need a license to keep the fish you catch."

"That's cool," I said. "Do you have a boat or anything?"

"No," Griffin said.

"Rats," I thought.

"But there are places where you can rent boats."

I brightened at that.

"At least, Dad can rent them," he added.

"Oh," I said, disappointed. My fantasy about spending my vacation on a boat in the river, like Huckleberry Finn, evaporated.

"Come on," Austin said, leading us off the dock to the river's edge. We explored along the shore, poking around with sticks.

"What do you guys do all summer," I asked.

"Play baseball, do stuff," Griffin said.

"Hang around here?" I said. "By the river?"

"Yeah, we hang out here a bit," answered Austin, "but mostly we play baseball."

"And you know what else?" Griffin said. "We've got season's tickets to the Winnipeg Goldeyes." He was grinning madly.

"What's that?" I said.

"Our baseball team. They play at Shaw Park. They're really good. You've got a season's ticket, too. It's a surprise."

It was a surprise all right. Baseball day and night. I had already told Griffin I didn't play baseball. I thought, "Wait until he sees why."

3 THE BIONIC BATTER

When I talked to my mom on the phone that night, I didn't tell her that she'd mistakenly sent me to Planet Baseball instead of Winnipeg. She had enough to worry about, considering she was going into the hospital the next day. Instead, I pumped her for info.

"So, Mom," I said, casually. "After they take out your brain, what do they replace it with?"

"Yours," she quipped, laughing.

"How long do you have to stay in the hospital after a brain transplant?" I asked.

"Not as long as you'd think."

That left me wondering if there was a joke in there or a bit of the truth. "So why do I have to stay out here all summer?"

"Because my new brain will need to be reprogrammed. It hasn't been used in a long, long time."

I could see we weren't going to get anywhere. It was my own fault for starting the joke, but I just couldn't come right out and ask her to tell me the truth. I'd thought it would be easier to talk about it over the phone, instead of in person, but it wasn't.

"Did Dad call?" I asked instead.

"No, I told him not to," she replied.

"Did you give him my number? So he can call me here?" I was sort of hoping that Mom's illness would bring Dad back from Florida. I'd hinted as much when I'd talked to him last. But he gave the same excuse as the one for why I couldn't go to stay with him in Orlando. He was on the road too much. He couldn't take the time off.

Later that night, as I lay in the bunk bed, I couldn't sleep. I was worried about my mom. I was also a little worried about these baseball fanatics I was living with. And most of all, I found it extremely disturbing to be surrounded by pictures of pitchers zeroing in on my noggin. Needless to say, I had some pretty wacky dreams.

After breakfast the next morning, Griffin and I went up to his room to play games on his computer and iPad. He let me use the iPad, showing me some great games we could play together, although I noticed that his favourites tended to be mostly sports-oriented. It turned out that Griffin also played hockey in the winter, so we had that in common at least. I played for a few years before my dad left town.

"You can download some of your own favourites, if you want to." Griffin said. I thought that was pretty decent of him. I hoped it meant I could go on the computer and iPad when I wanted to. He must have read my mind, because he said, "You can check your email on the iPad."

"Do you have a smart phone too?" I asked as he handed me the iPad. I figured with all that technology he probably had the latest phone. I was surprised by his answer.

"Naw. Texting is for girls. And the screen's too small for gaming."

"Right," I replied, reminding myself to use that excuse next time somebody asked me if I had one.

"Who's up for some throwing practice?" Andrew's voice boomed up the stairs.

"We're coming!" Griffin shouted back. Grabbing his glove and a ball from his trophy shelf, Griffin said, "Come on. This will be fun."

"Oh yeah," I thought, looking sadly at the computer. "This'll be so much better than surfing with a fast connection." Needless to say, I went.

I was a little surprised to see Claire packing a glove of her own. Andrew asked me, "Right or left?" while holding up two baseball gloves.

"I don't know," I said, although it didn't matter because I wasn't planning on participating.

"Never mind," said Andrew. "Take both."

Our little quartet walked up the street, greeting neighbours as we went. I had a little chuckle to myself when we passed the fake dog on a leash. The park with the red slide was pretty busy, with plenty of little kids crawling all over the playground.

We walked to an area I hadn't noticed when I'd been through the park with Griffin and Austin. There was a rough baseball diamond with a small fence behind home base. The diamond consisted mostly of ruts and the place for the pitcher was just a bit of a hump.

Griffin went immediately to the hump and Claire went off into the outfield where the cut grass ended at a field of high weeds. Andrew stood at home base with a glove and a bat beside him. I stood around on the sidelines, trying to look interested.

At first, Griffin just threw some pitches to his dad, who pretended he was catching for an imaginary batter.

"Strike," he called out to Griffin. "Nice one."

"Ball," he said when the pitch went high and away from the plate.

Claire got bored and wandered in to stand with me.

"Wanna play catch?" she asked me.

"Nah, I'll just watch." I replied.

"Okay," she said with a little shrug and sat down on the grass. I joined her because I was already tired of standing around.

Finally, after what seemed like a million pitches, Andrew called to Claire to go back to the outfield. He picked up the bat to face Griffin's first pitch. He missed. I don't know if he was really trying or not, but Griffin sure looked pleased.

Andrew pulled another ball out of what looked like a carpenter's tool belt around his waist. He tossed it to Griffin, who wasted no time firing it back at his dad. I don't think Andrew was quite ready because he missed that one too. This went on for as long as Andrew had balls. Then he went and picked up the balls he had missed, while Claire threw the only one he had hit to Griffin.

I was starting to doze off when I heard my name.

"What?" I mumbled, groggily.

"Do you want to catch?" Andrew was asking.

I was still half asleep. "Pardon?"

"I need a catcher. Would you mind?" Andrew held a glove out to me.

Reluctantly I took it. With the glove on my left hand, I felt like it was in a cast, just like it did the last time I tried to play baseball.

I didn't actually catch any balls. I just ran around behind Andrew to pick them up. At first I handed them back to Andrew to put into his ball belt, but soon he encouraged me to try throwing the ball to Griffin. I didn't want to disappoint him, but I couldn't get even one ball to go all the way to the mound.

I wanted to go back to handing Andrew the balls, but he and Griffin didn't seem to mind that I couldn't throw properly, so I just kept bouncing them out to Griffin. Claire had wandered in to second base, having seen very little action in the outfield. I guessed that

Griffin had gotten his baseball genes from his mother because his father couldn't hit the side of a barn with a school bus.

We took a little break to rest Griffin's arm. Claire begged me to play catch, so I reluctantly agreed to toss the ball to her. I made sure she stood only about as far away as I could throw the ball. After a few minutes, I got that eerie sensation that someone was looking at me. I turned around to see Andrew and Griffin eye-balling me.

"Connor, are you left-handed?" asked Andrew.

"No," I replied. "I mean, I write with my right hand, but I eat with my left."

"Why don't you try throwing with your left, then?" Andrew went to the pile of equipment and returned with a glove for my right hand. I put it on and it immediately felt better. Not entirely natural, but a lot less clunky.

However, when I threw the ball with my other arm it didn't feel much different, and I couldn't say that the ball went any farther. On the other hand — the one with the glove, that is — I caught the ball more easily. By the time I actually started getting the hang of things, Griffin went back up to the mound.

"Why don't you try hitting, Connor?" Andrew said.

"I don't know. I mean, okay." I couldn't do much worse than Andrew. He handed me the bat and told me to try hitting first from the right side, and then from the left. He told me I should stick with whichever side felt more natural to me.

I wasn't ready for the first pitch. Honest. It came too fast, crossing the plate before I could get the bat off my shoulder. Andrew spent a few minutes helping me with my stance. He explained that you don't actually rest the bat on your shoulder but hold it up in the air. That way I could be more prepared for the ball. It felt strange, standing there like the statue on top of a baseball trophy. With the next pitch, I got so caught up in holding my stance that the ball whistled right by — again. I started to get steamed.

Instead of throwing the ball back to Griffin, Andrew told him to take a break. "Hitting's a tricky business, Connor," Andrew explained. "There's a lot going on. The first thing you have to learn is to see the ball. It doesn't matter what you do with the bat if you can't see anything to hit."

It made some sense. But considering that I couldn't see the ball when I was just watching a game, how was I going to see it any better when I was playing? Then Andrew told me to drop the bat and to just stand beside the plate. He called out to Griffin, who was talking to Claire in the outfield.

"All right now, Connor," he instructed, "you just stand there and watch the ball. Try to follow it as it leaves Griffin's hand."

So I stood there staring intently at Griffin as he

wound up to pitch. I entirely missed seeing the first few pitches. I was still watching Griffin when I heard the ball hit the glove on Andrew's hand.

"Connor," Andrew said, "forget about Griffin. Right now he's just an arm and a hand with a ball in it. That's a million-dollar ball, it's your million-dollar ball. You don't want to let that ball out of your sight."

Thinking about the way Andrew described the ball got my imagination going. I tried to get into the million-dollar ball thing on the next pitch. I was surprised that I could follow its path across the plate. After that it got easier with each pitch.

"I'm ready," I announced, picking up the bat.

"Go for it, Connor," Andrew advised.

"Okay, Griffin," I shouted. "Show me the money."

The "hand" released the ball — it was coming at me. I had the bat up and I could feel my muscles tense as I leaned in. For a tiny second it was as though the ball was suspended in the air in front of me. I swung the bat around for all I was worth — hopefully, a million dollars.

I must have closed my eyes because I didn't see the ball leave the bat. I felt the impact in my hands and arms. Not sure what to do next, I just stood there, looking around. Andrew and Griffin were looking intently into the outfield where Claire was running back and forth along the border where the outfield ended and the area they called the "swamp" began.

"What happened?" I asked, confused.

Andrew laughed. "What happened? What happened? You nailed it. You hit it into the stratosphere!"

Meanwhile, Griffin went out to where Claire was still wandering around. After a few minutes, they both came back to the infield. "Can't find it," said Griffin. "It's in the swamp and the grass is too long."

"He hit it really far," added Claire. "It went over my head and then I lost it. Sorry, Dad."

I thought Andrew might be upset about losing a ball, but he was smiling when he said, "Too bad. It would have been nice for Connor to keep his first home run ball as a souvenir."

"Home run?" I had hit a home run! Wow! It felt pretty good, even without the ball.

"We've got plenty of baseballs," said Andrew. "That was a great pitch, Griffin."

"Yeah, great," replied Griffin, scowling a little as he made his way back to the mound.

"It was a great pitch," Andrew said to me. "But it was also a great hit. Let's see if you can do it again."

I was still thinking about my disappearing million-dollar ball. It didn't make a lot of sense to me, trying to knock your million dollars out of the park. On the other hand . . . Connor Wells, secret agent, stepped up to the plate. I had uncovered the plot to sabotage the World Series. Up on the mound, the pitcher, suspected international terrorist Dr. Spitball, readied what looked like a harmless baseball. In reality, however, it was . . . a bomb! The lives of my fans in the stands were at stake, not to mention my own. I had only one choice, to send that ball high into the stratosphere, where it would explode harmlessly. Fortunately, my new bionic arms were working perfectly.

I was ready. "Here it comes," I said, to myself. I swung the bat and felt that now familiar vibration. "And there it goes."

Relieved that I had saved the world from certain destruction, I dropped the bat. My work was done.

"Nice hit, Connor."

"Huh?" I said, in response.

"Another winner. Fortunately, Claire found it." Andrew put his hand on my shoulder and squeezed it. "How about another go, and this time, why don't you try running if you hit it?"

"Uh, okay." Secret agents are really smart guys. It was time to get back to work. Apparently Dr. Spitball had a few more bombs up his sleeves.

The pitch was right down the middle. I saw it clearly. Actually, I saw it clearly pass me as I swung at thin air. Fortunately for the world, it was a dud. Andrew threw it back to Dr. Spitball, who cracked an evil smile. "Ha!" he said. "Got you that time, smart guy."

I wasn't about to let that get to me. To the unsuspecting crowd it would appear that Dr. Spitball was using the same ball, but only I knew that he had switched it. I had noticed earlier that his hat was riding suspiciously high on his head. "How many balls has he got up there," I wondered.

We glared at each other. He squinted. "Here it comes," I repeated to myself. I had to give it to Dr. Spitball. It was another beauty pitch, but I had his number and it was zero! My heart leaped as the ball connected with the bat. It sailed out over Dr. Spitball's head. The crowd went wild. Little did they know that what they thought were fireworks was actually a bomb exploding halfway to the sun.

"Connor?" Andrew's voice woke me from my dream.

"Huh?" I said, using my all-purpose response.

"You're supposed to be running."

"Oh yeah. Should I go now?" I asked.

"Sure. Give it a try," he replied.

I put the bat down and ran for first base. It wasn't that far but I still only got going my fastest by the time I'd reached the indentation in the dirt that indicated the "bag." Unfortunately, I had a lot of trouble making the sharp left turn and ended up looping into the outfield on the way to second. The same thing happened again on the way to third and I was exhausted by the time I limped home.

"Your base running needs a little work," said Andrew. "But I think you've got the hitting down pretty well."

"Thanks," I said, feeling quite pleased with myself.

"That's all for today, kids." Andrew called to Griffin and Claire to come in.

Griffin was noticeably cooler toward me. Claire, on the other hand, embarrassed me with her praise.

"Nobody on Griffin's team can hit like that!" she gushed. Griffin's look got darker. I didn't really know what to say.

We gathered up the gear and left for home. Andrew and Griffin walked ahead, talking the whole way. I noticed that Andrew frequently put his arm around Griffin's shoulders. Meanwhile, Claire kept talking about my hitting, which continued to embarrass me. I'm not sure why. I should have been pleased, but I got the feeling that my success was at Griffin's expense. That didn't feel good at all.

4 JUST ONE OF THE FAMILY

I followed Griffin upstairs to his room because I couldn't think of anything else to do, but I was feeling pretty awkward, thinking that he was ticked off with me. He went straight to the computer and silently read his mail. I picked up one of his comic books and flopped onto the bed. We just hung around like that — me reading comics and Griffin surfing the internet — until dinner.

Dinner was at least six different dishes. Everybody grabbed something and helped themselves. Then the bowls and dishes got passed around until the plates were overflowing. I was glad to see that I wasn't the only one with a big appetite.

The second I put my fork into my mouth, Jane asked, "Did you have fun today, Connor?"

I was trying to chew and swallow fast to answer her, but Andrew jumped in. "I think Connor's been conning us," he said. "I bet you he's a Little League star in Burlington."

"No, I'm not," I protested. "I've never played baseball in my life!" I was lying. I'd played and failed miserably. My dad signed me up for T-ball when I was six. I couldn't even hit the ball when it was standing still. And in those days, the only thing I could throw was a tantrum. I stunk and I never went back.

Jane laughed. "Stop teasing him, Andrew." "Oh, I don't know. Nobody picks up a bat for the first time and hits a ball like that," Andrew replied.

"Like what?" asked Jane.

"Like José Bautista!" Andrew said.

"Prince Fielder!" Claire chimed in.

"Who?" I asked, confused.

Nobody bothered to answer me. Andrew and Claire gave Jane a play-by-play account of our afternoon. Griffin stayed mostly silent, except to say that none of his friends had ever hit a ball into the swamp.

"I'm telling you, Jane," said Andrew. "Connor hits the ball better than anyone on Griffin's team and he says he's never played baseball. Right, Connor?"

I kept my mouth shut.

Jane looked at Griffin, who was just pushing his food around on his plate. "I hope you weren't pushing Griffin too hard, Andrew. He practised a lot last week."

"No, Griffin was pitching fine. Great, in fact. That's just it. He was throwing hard and fast. Most kids couldn't hit him. They wouldn't even see the ball."

That perked Griffin up. "Dad says Connor has a really good eye. He sees the ball really well."

"I do?" I said.

"Well you hit it, didn't you?" laughed Griffin. He broke into a big grin and I could see that he wasn't mad any more.

"Lots," said Claire. Then we all laughed.

Later, Griffin followed Jane into the kitchen and emerged carrying two plates of pie with ice cream. He put one in front of me. "Thanks," I said. The pie was warm and it smelled sooo good.

Over dessert, the conversation started up again. This time they talked about painting the house. "I think colonial blue would be nice for a change," said Jane.

"Then it won't match the cars," replied Andrew.

"Oh for heaven's sake, Andrew. The house paint doesn't always have to match the cars. We have the only house in Rivergrove with matching cars and house trim."

"I like it that way," Andrew said.

"Well, I'm tired of green and I want blue." Jane took a bite of pie.

I thought maybe this was the start of an argument, but Andrew didn't seem to be too upset. "Well," he said. "We'll just have to get new cars."

Jane laughed. "Forget it, pal. You want matching cars, you'll just have to paint them. Paint's cheaper."

Andrew grumbled, good-naturedly, "I don't like blue cars."

"Let's vote on it," Jane replied. "All in favour?" She quickly grabbed Claire's and Griffin's arms and raised them over their heads. "Three to one," she declared. "Connor, care to weigh in?"

"I'm out of it," I replied quickly, not wanting to take sides.

"Blue it is. I'll pick up the paint tomorrow."

"Yuck," Andrew groaned, while the rest of the family laughed. "I think I'll go to my room and sulk."

I was thinking, through the entire conversation, about how different it was having dinner with a family like the Campbells. Different from at home, I mean. Even when my dad was still around, it was usually just Mom and me at suppertime because Dad travelled so much. We didn't talk much, and often we just sat in front of the TV, eating from trays. That got me thinking about my mom and suddenly I blurted out loudly, "What's wrong with my mom?"

Everyone turned to look at me. "I beg your pardon, Connor?" Jane said.

"I was just wondering if you know what's wrong with my mom," I stammered, a little embarrassed. "She never actually said what she has."

Jane shot Andrew a look before she answered me. "Well, Connor," she said, slowly. "I can't say that we know the exact nature of the problem ourselves."

"Oh," was all I could think of to say.

"But she's not going to be in the hospital very long,"

Jane added, hastily.

"Then how come I have to be away for the whole summer?"

Andrew piped in, "That was my idea, actually. I thought you might enjoy spending the summer in a new place and we were very keen to get to know you."

I wondered if Andrew was just bluffing, because what he said sounded kind of gushy.

"Even minor operations take a long time to recover from," said Jane. "Andrew had his gall bladder out three years ago and he's still not over it."

Everybody laughed at that except me, especially because I didn't know what a gall bladder was. "So she's having an operation?" I said.

"Well, that was just an example, Connor." Jane went on, "We don't have all the details. I'm sure your mother will let us know more as things progress. Your grandparents will take good care of her and you have nothing to worry about."

"Yeah, right," I thought. They hadn't seen how thin and pale she was. "Would Jane and Andrew lie to me?" I wondered.

Jane stood up and grabbed some plates off the table. Griffin, Claire, and Andrew followed her to the kitchen, which put an end to the discussion. I sat there for a few more seconds before I picked up my plate and followed them.

After we finished clearing the table, Griffin and I

watched some television. Even though it was summer holidays for them, Griffin explained, the kids still had to be in their rooms by ten o'clock. The family tried to keep up their regular weekly routine, especially meal times.

"That's because my mom works at home and she says it's too disruptive if we all get up and eat breakfast at different times."

"What does she do — for work, I mean," I asked.

Griffin replied, "She's an event planner."

"What's that?" I'd never heard of that job before.

"She, um, well," Griffin said "plans . . ."

"Events?" I finished for him.

"Yeah, that's it," he laughed. "Come on, let's go up to our room and check our messages."

It was funny hearing him refer to it as "our room." I've never had to share my room or my stuff because I'm an only child. Of course, I wasn't sharing with him — he was sharing with me.

"Go ahead," he said, indicating the computer.

I sat down and logged on. I knew that Griffin had sent me a message earlier in the day, but that wasn't the only one I had. There were two other unread messages. One was from Austin and the other from someone named D.J. I turned around to find Griffin grinning behind me.

It took me forever to tap out replies. My typing skills were pretty bad, even though I'd had plenty of practice in school.

"Your dad's a pretty crappy hitter," I said as we played a baseball video game later.

Griffin laughed. "Not really. He just doesn't try."

"Why not? It's fun hitting the ball." I couldn't believe I'd said that — "Baseball" and "fun" in the same sentence. Weird.

"'Cause he's watching my pitches, the strike zone, the speed — stuff like that. Besides, he's a lot taller than the kids I pitch to, and it's hard to hit balls around your ankles."

"Maybe he should be using a golf club." I grinned.

We had a good laugh at that.

5 BASEBALL BOOT CAMP

Griffin woke me up by stepping on my arm as he got out of his bunk.

"Ow!" I hollered.

"Ow!" he hollered too, as he slipped and tumbled onto the floor with a thud.

"What's going on up there?" Jane's voice drifted up from her office below us.

Griffin didn't bother to answer her. He just scrambled into his clothes and dashed down the hall to the bathroom. I could hear water running and the sounds of vigorous tooth-brushing.

I pulled on shorts and a T-shirt and followed Griffin to the bathroom. The door was open and Griffin was wetting his hair down with water at one of the two sinks. He wasn't very successful in flattening it out. It stood up in spikes all over his head. For once, I was glad I had curly hair.

Griffin poked his head into his mother's office on our way to the kitchen. "We're cool, Mom," he said.

"We don't need any help."

"What was going on up there?" Jane asked.

"Nothing," Griffin replied. "Connor fell out of bed."

"Hey," I protested.

"Are you all right, Connor?" Jane asked, concerned.

"Yeah, I'm fine," I replied, forgetting that it wasn't me who'd fallen.

All the breakfast things were out on the table and the counter. We helped ourselves to cereal and juice. Before his first bite, Griffin was dialling the phone. His conversations were brief. It sounded like he was setting something up with his friends.

"Okay, dude," he said, after he had wolfed down two bowls of cereal, "time to split."

"For where?" I asked.

"Where else?" he laughed, picking up his glove, balls, and bats from the mud room. He tossed me the bag of balls and I dropped it. "I hope you get picked for the other team," he commented. "I'll hit every pitch out to you."

I followed him out the door and down the street, where we stopped at Austin's place to pick him up. There were already six guys at the baseball diamond when we arrived. Griffin introduced me to everybody. I couldn't remember their names and it just got worse when four more guys arrived.

Those kids were really organized. They tossed a coin to pick teams, with Griffin as the captain of one.

He won the toss and immediately picked me for his team. Big mistake, now I'd be fumbling the other team's hits. But, it felt better than being left to last. That honour went to Austin, which I thought sucked, but he took it well.

"I stink," he said as he joined our side.

"Yeah?" I replied. "Well, you ain't seen nothin' yet."

We were six kids per team. That left one guy who wasn't included when they chose sides. I looked at Griffin and pointed at the short, red-haired kid. "What gives?"

"Matt's the catcher," he explained. "He plays for both teams, but he doesn't get any at-bats."

"Why not?" I asked.

"Because he sucks!" cried Austin. "He's worse than me."

The other guys laughed at that. We were the "home" team today, so that meant that we were on the field first. That also meant that I had absolutely no idea what to do. Griffin went into a huddle with the five other players and when it was over he pointed between second and third bases and said, "Left field. You should be okay out there. Nobody ever hits that far."

That pretty much told the other guys I was completely useless on the field. Everybody was pairing up and tossing a ball back and forth. Because Griffin was practising with Matt, I was the odd man out. I tossed a ball straight up in the air and tried catching it, but on every toss the ball travelled far to the right or left or behind and I didn't catch one. After a while, I figured Austin took pity on me because he tossed me a ball.

Austin's throws seemed to be all over the place. I had to stretch my arms and my body to try to stop the ball, but I kept falling over.

"Austin," I said, "are you throwing to me or somebody else?"

Austin just laughed and threw another loopy ball over my head.

For my part, I was so exhausted chasing after the ball that I barely had the energy to throw back to Austin. Sometimes I just bowled it back to him, an approach that was more accurate than when I threw. Most of my throws fell short, but not by too much.

"You throw like your arms are wet noodles," said Austin, loud enough to turn a few heads. I saw some smirks.

"You throw like an alien," I retorted. I didn't know how aliens threw, but I knew for certain that we both stunk.

"Watch me," Austin said, flinging his arm way back. He completed his throwing motion but didn't release the ball. "See that?" he said. "That's how you're supposed to throw. Now watch how you do it."

He brought his arm up, waggled it in the air, flexed his wrist and let the ball plop down at his feet. He looked ridiculous.

"I do not throw like that," I shouted.

"Well maybe not exactly like that," he said, "but you still throw from your elbow."

Great, I thought, I'm getting lessons from the team doofus. Fortunately, my lesson came to an end as Matt yelled, "Let's play ball!"

I trotted out to left field, hoping that Griffin wasn't lying about how busy I'd be. I checked out Austin in right field, who was just standing there like I was, shading his eyes with his glove.

Griffin put the first two batters away easily. I figured we'd be off the field in quick order. Ha! I heard that unmistakable sound of ball hitting bat and started looking around wildly. Griffin was yelling my name and pointing in the air over my head. I looked up, but all I could see was sun. I was still looking up when I heard a soft thud behind me.

Swinging around, I spied the ball in the grass only a metre away. I grabbed it but then realized I had no idea what to do with it. Was I supposed to run with it? "No," I thought, "that's football."

"Throw, throw," the rest of my teammates chanted.

"Okay!" I yelled back. But where? The player on third base was gesturing like a madman. I figured that since he was closest I should throw the ball to him. I lifted my arm and suddenly I had a vision of Austin mimicking me. I jerked my arm back and flailed it, releasing the ball. The motion was so violent, I thought my arm fell off.

The ball plopped down halfway between me and the third baseman. I ran at it, my head down. Reaching for the ball, I was knocked off my feet as I collided with the third baseman. We both ended up rolling around on the ground. I could hear a cheer from behind me. I guessed that the runner had scored — thanks to me.

"Hey, I'm sorry," I said, as I helped the other kid up. He was about half my size.

"It's okay," he replied. "Griffin said you don't know how to play. I should have told you I was running for it." I could hear the rest of the guys laughing at us.

"Watch where you walk. I dropped my glasses," he added, looking around.

"Why don't you watch where you walk, and I'll look for them," I replied.

I found his glasses a couple of feet away. Fortunately, they weren't broken. I handed them to him and walked back to my position.

The game got back underway and thankfully, the inning was over on the next pitch. I was grateful that the ball was hit back to the mound where Griffin caught it effortlessly.

My team huddled on the sidelines to discuss batting order. "Connor should bat third," Griffin suggested.

"I hope he hits better than he fields," commented the third baseman.

"If he was any worse, he'd be Austin," somebody else said. Everybody laughed at that, including Austin.

"I'll go first," said Griffin, "and Connor can go after D.J."

"As long as he doesn't run me over again," replied D.J., the third baseman I'd collided with.

"D.J.," said Austin, "a turtle could outrun you."

I thought these guys were pretty hard on each other, but nobody seemed to take the teasing too seriously.

"I'm not so fast myself, D.J.," I said, keeping quiet about my hitting. I didn't want to set myself up for a fall. After all, what if yesterday had been a fluke?

Matt trotted over to us from home plate. "Are you guys going to play ball or what?" We broke it up and Griffin picked up a bat.

He took a couple of practice swings, pointed the bat at the pitcher and took up position. The first pitch was in the dirt, rolling to the backstop. Matt yelled, "Ball one!"

The pitcher scowled. His next pitch was closer to the mark and Griffin smacked it over the first baseman's head. It didn't roll far, just far enough to allow Griffin to reach first.

D.J. stood up and marched up to the plate. He didn't bother with practice swings. Maybe he should have, because he went down swinging on three pitches. I passed him on my way to the plate. "Kevin's hot today," was all he said.

I was so nervous, I swung the bat long before the pitch crossed the plate. I heard a couple of snickers behind me. "Strike one," shouted Matt. I wished Andrew was behind me. I tried to remember what he had told me, but most of it went right out of my head.

"You get three strikes," Matt added.

"Thanks," I replied. "I knew that. Everybody knows that."

"Okay, just checking," Matt said.

I let the next pitch go by. This got the boys snickering again, but I had a plan. I needed to see the ball. Just like yesterday, see it first, hit it second. I was dimly aware of Matt's vigorous "Strike two!"

Over on first base, Griffin gave me a thumbs-up. I lifted the bat off my shoulder. Leaning over the plate, I fastened my eyes onto the hand clutching the ball. The ball left the hand and travelled toward me. At first it looked like it was going to be a winner, but it dipped dramatically, forcing Matt to reach under me to catch it. The laughing was abruptly cut off by Matt's assessment of the situation. "BALL ONE!" he shouted.

I was getting anxious to take a swing. The pitcher took his time, testing my concentration. I didn't look around, I just stared. Finally, he released the ball. "That's more like it!" I thought, bringing the bat back. I got under it and sent it back out over the pitcher's head. It kept going, over the outfield and into the swamp.

"Hey, are you waiting for your pinch runner, or what?" asked Matt.

"Huh?" I replied. "Oh yeah." I dropped the bat and

raced like a madman for first base. No fear of my over-running Griffin. I was pumping but not making a lot of ground. Finally, I huffed across home plate. My teammates crowded around me.

"Awesome hit, Connor," said Austin.

"Where'd you learn to hit like that?" asked D.J.

"Griffin's dad taught me," I said. "Yesterday."

"No way!"

"Way!"

D.J. turned on Griffin. "I thought you said he'd never played before."

"He hasn't," Griffin retorted. "He's telling the truth. My dad taught him yesterday."

I kept my mouth shut. We had all that time for chit-chat because the members of the other team were wandering around in the swamp looking for the ball. Matt, looking bored, came over to join us.

"Nice hit," he said to me. "Remember, you're supposed to run when you do that."

"Oh yeah?" I said. "To where?"

6 BAT OF STEEL, ARM OF RUBBER

I figured that if I was going to be stuck in baseball boot camp for the summer, I'd better make the most of it. I didn't get another chance to hit in that inning. Austin and the first baseman popped up, ending our inning.

Putting on that glove again didn't feel any better than before. Maybe I needed gloves on both hands. Then I could boot the ball into the infield with my feet. I'd probably be more accurate that way.

While I pondered that possibility, D.J. let a ground ball through on my side. I hesitated, not wanting a repeat of our earlier collision, but D.J. was yelling at me, "Pick it up, pick it up, PICK IT UP!"

"Oh great," I thought, "here I go again." Then I ran right past the ball. I could hear the hoots and hollers from my teammates as I put it in reverse. I grabbed the ball, shut my eyes, and hurled it with all my might. Instead of throwing the ball into the infield, I got turned around and threw it far into centre field. Austin, who was guarding right field looked completely surprised as the ball bounced on the edge of his turf.

By the time he got to it and fired it in, the runner was already home. Austin fell, rolling on the grass, laughing and holding his sides. I felt pretty stupid yelling "Sorry!" to someone who was convulsed in laughter.

Griffin walked out to see me. He had a goofy grin on his face and he was obviously trying not to laugh out loud. His attempt failed and he just stood there in front of me, guffawing loudly. When I got over my initial embarrassment, I joined him. Without their pitcher to keep the game going, the rest of the team had nothing to do, so they all wandered over.

"Man, oh man," snickered Austin, "you stink, Connor."

I had to agree with him.

"But he sure can hit," added Griffin.

Everyone agreed with that.

Eventually, the other side grew impatient with us, sending Matt out once again to get us back on track.

Before Griffin headed back to the mound, he said, "Just run with the ball, toward D.J. or Vincent, on second. When you get close enough, lob the ball, underhand."

Pretty pathetic. I needed my own personal pinch runner, pinch catcher, and pinch thrower. Every time Griffin pitched a ball at the plate, I cringed. Fortunately, we got out of it when the next three batters went down swinging.

Vincent, our second baseman, was up first. He managed a good hit on the second pitch, reaching first base easily. He held there as Griffin went up to bat for the second time. Griffin let two good pitches go by — strikes called by Matt. They had a friendly dispute over the second one, but Matt wouldn't reverse his decision.

I wasn't quite sure what Griffin was doing when he turned his body slightly toward the pitcher and slid his hand down the bat. I had expected a big swing. The ball rolled gently off the bat toward third base. Griffin took off like a shot for first base. Vincent arrived at second and all were safe.

"Nice bunt, Grif," shouted D.J. The other guys grunted their appreciation of Griffin's mini-hit.

Then D.J. struck out and I was up again with two men on.

"Bring 'em home, Connor," Austin instructed. He had a really serious look on his face, which was a complete turnaround from his usual grin. It was a tall order, considering that I still felt pretty useless.

"Yeah, sure," I said, as I wandered over to the plate and picked up the bat that Griffin had dropped there.

I looked out at Kevin on the mound, slitting my eyes. "Okay, Colonel Curveball," I said to myself. "Just try and get me." Once again, I let the first ball go by. Matt caught it easily, but in my mind it was a lethal ballstar. Ballstars look like ordinary baseballs to unsuspecting citizens. Little do they know that ballstars sprout lacerating wings that tear through a guy like a laser through butter. Fortunately for Matt, he was not Colonel Curveball's target. I had to be constantly careful because my slightly magnetic bionic parts attracted ballstars.

"Uh, Connor," said Matt, interrupting my fantasy. "You planning on taking any more pitches?"

"Huh," I said.

"You won't hit anything standing there with the bat at your feet," he replied.

"Oh, yeah," I said, lifting the bat.

"Hit me," I yelled to Colonel Curveball, alias Kevin. "As if," I said to myself.

The ballstar left the Colonel's hand at the speed of light. Fortunately, my bionic eyes could see it clearly. I waited. And watched it sail into the backstop behind me. It was a good thing for the world and secret agents like me that Colonel Curveball was such a lousy pitcher.

The next ball looked good all the way to within a metre of the plate, where it dipped precariously. It dribbled over my shoes, rolling harmlessly into Matt's glove.

I was starting to wonder how anyone could strike out against Kevin, that is, the Colonel. Then he let loose a winner.

It was a beauty, coming at supersonic speed, waist high. I swung my detonator, launching the ballstar into the swamp, where it wouldn't hurt anybody.

"Run," Matt hissed behind me.

I flung the bat wildly and took off for first. I was so

engrossed in watching them hunt for the ball that I missed second base altogether, or so they told me. "Go back," Griffin shouted. "Connor, go back and touch second."

It took me a good few steps to stop and make the 180-degree return to second. Then I overran it and had to do another awkward 180. I was a lot more careful rounding third. In fact, I almost slowed to a walk, stepped onto it, pivoted, and broke into a trot for home. It wasn't pretty.

"A three-run shot!" someone said.

"Five to two," crowed Austin, "we're creaming them."

"Man, how do you do that?" asked Kale.

I wasn't about to tell him about Colonel Curveball and the rest of it, so I just shrugged. To tell the truth, I didn't really know myself.

The rest of the game was pretty much the same. I flubbed and fumbled in the outfield on the few occasions that balls got through the two basemen. But when it came to hitting balls, I was able to hit into the swamp virtually every time. I could tell the other team was ticked. We won the game twelve runs to three. I drove in ten of them. Not a bad day's work.

Afterwards, most of the guys from both teams went down to the river. While we sat on the dock, D.J. said, "We could use Connor on the team." Griffin, Austin, and Matt agreed. I was confused. I thought I was already on their team.

It became clearer when Griffin said to me, "What do you think, Connor? Do you want to try out for the Spinners?" It took me a couple of seconds but then I remembered that "Spinners" was the name of his Little League team.

Considering how badly I had played in the field, I was totally surprised that they would ask me, but I figured, "What the heck — it might even be fun." So I said yes.

Big mistake.

7 HIT AND MISS

Griffin's next practice was on Wednesday, which was also the first day that I would be able to talk to my mom in the hospital. She was going to be really surprised when I told her that I was playing baseball.

Griffin and Claire helped me practise my hitting. After Claire complained that she was tired of searching through the weeds for balls, Griffin turned around on the mound and I hit from the outfield into the backstop. That cut down on the number of balls Claire had to chase. Of course, I missed a lot and had to wade into the weeds myself to retrieve the balls.

"We need a batting cage," Griffin said, during a break.

"What's that?" I inquired.

"It's like a bowling alley for hitting baseballs. There's a machine that shoots balls at you and you hit them into a net. They have one at Shaw Park."

"Cool," I said, although I was thinking it didn't sound like such a hot idea, letting a machine fire balls at you. "Maybe we could go practice there."

Griffin laughed. "I wish," he said.

After an early dinner on Wednesday, we picked up Austin and went to a baseball diamond at a high school. A whole bunch of kids and adults were already there. D.J. and Vincent came over to see us, while Andrew went off to talk to some adults who I guessed were the coaches.

"You don't have to be nervous," Griffin said. "It's only a practice."

"I'm not nervous," I replied. Actually, I was a little, but not about hitting.

Griffin went off to warm up when Matt arrived. I kind of lurked around on the sidelines, waiting for Andrew to come back.

"Connor!" I heard my name being called and looked around to see Andrew waving me over.

"Connor, meet Coach Gelber and Coach Markovic," Andrew said, indicating the two men.

"Andrew tells us you swing a pretty big bat," said Coach Gelber. "How 'bout you show us what can you do?"

I nodded as Coach Markovic handed me a bat. I figured that it would be Griffin pitching to me, but another kid I'd never seen before was on the mound. He was as tall as me, but really skinny. He didn't look like he had the strength to throw the ball at all, so I was surprised when he threw hard across the plate. I whiffed it so bad that I almost fell into the dirt. I saw

Coach Markovic and Coach Gelber exchange glances.

Andrew said, "Settle down, Connor, don't try to kill the ball."

Actually, that's exactly what I was trying to do. It usually worked. I got back into position for the next pitch, which looked a little low, so I let it slide. I didn't turn around, but I guessed the coaches were giving each other looks again. The kid on the mound was getting all smirky and I didn't like that. "I'll wipe that smirk off your face, pal," I said to myself. "Just get that ball close and I'll do the rest."

He did, and I gave it everything I had. I wasn't sure if I was supposed to run around the bases, so I just stood there watching the ball sail away.

The kids on the field stopped what they were doing. A few pointed to it as the ball flew over their heads. I looked over at the coaches. They were looking into the field too. Andrew was smiling at me, giving me a thumbs-up.

Coach Gelber came over to me. "Think you can do that again?" he asked.

"Yeah, I think so." "Sir," I added.

"Let's do it, Ty!" he called out to the mound. The pitcher's head swivelled in our direction. The coach tossed him a ball. "Connor, when you hit the ball next time, I'd like to see you run the bases."

"Uh, oh!" I thought. "This could be trouble."

Fortunately, the next ball I hit followed the first

one into outer space. I loped around the bases casually. When I arrived at home plate, Coach Gelber was waiting for me. "You're hitting well, Connor. But I'd like to see you put some hustle into your base running."

A few pitches later, I hit a grounder past Ty. In my haste to hustle, I tripped myself with the bat. Stumbling along the base line, I made it to first base a few seconds after the ball. Coach Gelber waved me back to home plate.

Another ground ball, this time into left field, meant that I would have to hoof it around the bases again. Fortunately, this time I didn't get tangled up in the bat. Instead, I tripped over the bag and sprawled into the grass. My face plant brought on howls of laughter from the other kids. I could hear Austin's crowing above the rest.

When I picked myself up off the grass, I was relieved to see the coaches were waving me over to them. Andrew came out to meet me halfway. "That went well, I think," he said kindly.

"Yeah, right," I snorted. "If they need somebody to pick weeds with their teeth, I'm their guy."

Andrew just laughed. I dreaded facing the coaches, but they didn't seem too concerned about my swan dive. "Do you have a glove, Connor?" Coach Markovic asked.

"Yeah," I replied, pointing to it.

"Let's play a little catch," he said.

We stood a short distance apart. I found the ball easy to catch, but I kept freezing up on my throws. Only one in five came within arm's length of the coach. Every few pitches, Coach Markovic took a couple of steps back, until he was just too far for me to ever hope reaching him with a ball. He was throwing harder too. I missed more than I caught. Mercifully, he cut the torture off. "That's fine, Connor," he said, without conviction. "I'd like you to go into the out-field with Austin and Kirby, and try fielding some balls I'm going to hit out there. You catch what you can, chase down what you can't, and throw to the nearest baseman. Is that clear?"

"Yeah," I thought, "basically, run around like a chicken with my head cut off." Which is exactly what I did. I spent most of the time looking vainly into the sky for a glimpse of the ball. When I did see it, I couldn't catch it. And when I chased it, I kicked it farther away. Needless to say, I didn't have to do a lot of throwing. I never actually got my hands on a ball.

All the good feelings I'd had when I hit those balls had evaporated. When they finally called me in, Andrew was standing alone and he wasn't wearing his usual smile.

"I know," I said, before he could drop the news on me. "I stink."

"I wish I had better news, Connor. They were very impressed with your hitting. There isn't another kid on this team who can hit like you do. It's like I told you at

Griffin's game the other day. They don't have designated hitters. Players need to be able to play positions as well."

Andrew's voice sounded like he was sad for me and I appreciated that. But it didn't make me feel any less humiliated. I realized he was still talking.

"They said you could sit on the bench with the team, and maybe play an inning once in a while."

"Whoopee," I mumbled. I was sorry I'd let them talk me into this. I mumbled something even I couldn't make out.

"I beg your pardon, Connor?" Andrew asked.

"I'm going to get some water," I said, pointing to a big water jug sitting on the end of the bench.

I wandered over to the water jug and poured some into a plastic cup. The team was busy practising. Everyone else was busy watching, including Andrew.

I was ticked off, so I decided to take a little walk to let off some steam.

There wasn't much to see around the school, and I wasn't sightseeing anyway, so I left the grounds. I thought I'd just walk around the block a time or two, but the street wound around a bit and after a while I kind of lost track of time and direction. Now I wouldn't have anything exciting to tell my mom. What was I going to say? "Things are going great out here, Mom. Everybody's real nice but I stink at baseball." In the real world that would be okay, but out here in Baseball Land, I was a total loser. If she was going to send me to a parallel universe, why couldn't it have been Video Game World?

I told myself that it wasn't my idea to get involved in baseball, and I shouldn't be so upset that it didn't work out. But the truth is, I wanted to play on the team with Griffin and my new friends. I got that old T-ball feeling, all over again.

Eventually, I realized it was getting dark. I didn't have a watch on, so I didn't know how long I'd been gone. At that point it didn't matter, because I also realized I had no idea where I was. At first I wasn't worried, as I hadn't gone far. At least I didn't think I had. Then, after walking around for another few minutes while the sun set, I knew I was hopelessly lost. Imagine my relief when I saw a convenience store.

I rushed up to the store but when I got there, there wasn't a public phone. I asked the guy behind the counter if I could use the phone. He looked me over pretty carefully before nodding. "Just give me the number and I'll dial it," he said. Right. Now, I had a problem.

"Uh, I don't have the number with me," I said.

"You got a name and address I can look up for you?" The clerk took a cellphone out of his pocket.

"Yeah, of course," I said, momentarily relieved. That is until I started wracking my brain for Griffin's last name. I just stood there, my mind a total blank. "Never mind," I said, and went outside where I sat on the sidewalk to think. That's where I was a few minutes later when the guy stuck his head out the door.

"You okay, kid?" he asked.

I wasn't okay. I felt like a complete doofus and I really didn't want to tell him my problem. Finally I overcame my reluctance and told him what happened.

"Come on inside," he said. "I'll call the police. They know what to do."

Yipes! Now I'd have something to tell Mom. Except it wasn't exactly the kind of news she'd like to hear — that her kid is a lousy baseball player AND a big dope. A patrol car arrived in a short time. I had to relate my tale of woe to the officers. It went like this:

THEM: "Do you know the name of the family you're staying with?"

ME: "No."

THEM: "Do you know the name of the street where they live?"

ME: "No."

THEM: "Do they live on this side of the highway?"

ME: "I don't know."

Genius. One of the officers went back to the patrol car, while the other chatted with the store clerk. I wandered around the aisles feeling like a dummy.

"Don't worry, kid," said the officer. "Your relatives will probably call the station about you and then we'll have you home in a jif."

A jif. Whatever that was. I glanced up over the top of a shelf full of soup cans. The red and white labels jump-started my brain. "Campbell!" I yelled loudly, waving a can of tomato soup. "Campbell, their name is Campbell. Andrew and Jane CAMPBELL!"

The clerk and the officer laughed out loud. I joined them, laughing in relief. The officer went outside and within moments was back. "Okay, kid," he said, grinning. "Let's get you home."

I thanked the store clerk, hopped into the back of the car and actually enjoyed the short trip. The car had a cool computer screen and they let me listen to the police radio.

When we arrived at the Campbells' house, they were all standing on the front lawn. The policeman had to let me out of the back seat because there aren't any door handles back there. I noticed more people spilling out of their houses.

Everybody started talking to me at once, saying that they were worried, asking if I was okay and if I was hungry. Andrew thanked the police officers and we went inside where Jane had set out some snacks on the kitchen table.

"I'm going to get Connor a dog tag ID tomorrow. We'll put our address and phone numbers on it, so he won't have any trouble finding us again," Jane announced. She looked at Andrew. "Maybe we should get him a cellphone while he's here." She didn't wait for Andrew to answer. "Yes, that's a much better idea."

I couldn't believe my ears. Do something stupid like getting lost and you get a cellphone. Inside my head, I could hear my mother saying, "That's far too generous. You don't need it, say thank you and that the dog tag will be just fine." Instead, I said, "Maybe I should just memorize your address and phone number." Mom would be proud.

Nobody said anything about what had happened at the baseball practice, and they kept blaming themselves because I got myself lost.

By then, it was too late to call my mom. I was really sorry that I'd let her down, and now I'd probably have to tell her why I hadn't called. I started working on my alien abduction excuse.

8 TARGET PRACTICE

The next morning, Griffin didn't say a word about the tryout catastrophe. He was acting extra nice to me, which I took to mean that he felt sorry for me. I didn't want his pity. I didn't NEED his pity. When he headed for the door after breakfast, collecting his baseball things, he must have assumed I was behind him because he went out and came right back in. I had poured another bowl of cereal.

"Are you coming, Connor?" he asked.

"Nah," I replied, casually. "I'm a little 'baseballed' out."

Griffin looked like he was going to say something, then changed his mind. He shrugged and went back out the door. I ate cereal — very slowly. After a few minutes, I realized that I hadn't asked him if I could use his computer. Bummer.

Claire wandered down as I was finishing my breakfast, so I stayed and ate some more with her. "Where's Griffin?" she asked.

"Gone to play baseball with his friends," I replied.

"How come you didn't go with him?" she asked.

"Didn't feel like it," I answered.

"Oh." Claire put some bread in the toaster. "Wanna play Xbox with me?"

"Okay," I said, thinking it was better than eating breakfast all day.

Before we got a chance to rev up the TV, Jane came into the kitchen.

"Where's Griffin?" she asked.

"Playing baseball," Claire answered.

"Oh." Jane looked at me quickly, then turned away. "What do you kids say we go to the mall and get Connor that phone?

"Yeah!" Claire said.

When we got to the mall, Jane took us directly to the phone store. While I drooled over the smart phones, Jane and the sales guy looked at old-school flip phones. "Hey, it's better than no phone," I thought.

When they were done, Jane handed me my phone. "It's a basic handset, no text or data," she said. "But our number is programmed and we can call you if you remember to keep it turned on."

A phone that was only for talking. I wondered what Griffin would think of that. I thanked Jane and hoped she could see how grateful I was for their help.

On our way through the mall, we passed an engraving place and Claire stopped to look at the dog tags.

"Look Connor," she said, "just like the soldiers have." She was right, I hadn't thought of that. They did look kind of cool. "Can we get them too, Mom?" Claire asked.

"Don't you know your address either, Claire?" I joked.

She shot me a look and said, "What if I get amnesia?"

"Yeah, right," I taunted.

"It could happen," she said pouting.

Jane and the sales clerk laughed at that. "I think that's a great idea, Claire." Jane said. "You never know when you might be struck by lightning or something," she added.

Claire stuck her tongue out at me. Considering the amount of time that family spent outdoors, it was a good possibility.

Jane bought Claire, Griffin, and me each a tag with a chain. "There, if you all get hit by lightning at the same moment, they'll know where to send you."

On the way home, Jane got a text from Griffin saying that he was going to Austin's house for lunch. He must have been pretty ticked off at me, although I don't see why he should have been. You'd think he would have invited me to lunch. Just because I didn't want to play baseball didn't mean I wouldn't eat lunch. Oh well, I had soup and sandwiches with Jane and Claire.

After lunch, Claire and I went into the family room to watch videos. A while later, Jane came in and suggested we go outside to play for a while. I looked at

Claire, thinking it was pretty strange to go out to "play" with a little girl.

"Don't you have any friends to play with?" I asked Claire.

"Of course I do," she stated. "I just wanted to hang with you today."

I laughed at the way she said that.

"Okay dude, let's hang. What do you want to do?" I asked.

"We could play catch," she replied, brightly.

"I don't feel like playing baseball today," I countered.

"Not baseball, just catch," she said. "I need the practice. Please?"

What choice did I have? My new BFF wanted to play catch.

We went into the backyard and took up stations beside the flower beds at opposite ends of the lawn.

"What happens if I miss and it goes into the garden?" I asked.

"Go get it. Just don't step on the flowers," Claire replied.

I looked into the densely packed flower bed. There were a few little stepping stones, but otherwise the entire thing was covered in flowers. I really hoped I wouldn't need to go in there. Maybe I would just send Claire.

Claire tossed the first ball, not hard, but right on the money. I shot my hand out to grab it, but I only succeeded in knocking it down. I saw Claire frown.

"Connor, throw me the ball and then watch me catch it," she said.

I did just that, not quite as accurately as she had, but close enough for her to get to it. I watched her and didn't see anything special going on.

"See how I put my other hand up to the glove to keep the ball from falling out?" she asked.

I hadn't noticed. She rolled the ball back to me and told me to throw again. This time I did see what she meant.

"You've got to watch the ball go into your glove. Turn your body. Don't just stand there with your arm stuck out."

"Well, thank you, little Miss Baseball," I thought. "Okay," I said, out loud. "Fire it here."

She lobbed me another ball, a little off to my right. I had to lean way over. At the last moment I remembered to trap the ball in my glove with my left hand. It worked. The ball stayed in there.

"Now throw it back," Claire shouted. "Right away, quick!"

I snatched the ball out of my glove and spun around to hurl the ball back as she requested. Unfortunately, I fired it right into the back wall of the garage.

Claire got a big chuckle out of that. She walked over to retrieve the ball, saying over her shoulder, "You can't just stand there after you catch the ball, you know. You have to throw it."

"Well, excuse me," I retorted. "I thought we were just playing catch."

"I'm playing catch," she corrected. "You're learning to play catch."

"Whoa!" I thought. Claire could be a bossy kid when she wanted to. "How come you know so much about it?" I asked.

"Because I go to all the practices and games. And I play on a softball team," she replied, tartly.

I guessed that I had that to look forward to. Baseball games with a bunch of little girls. Maybe I should have checked to see if Andrew and Jane played as well.

"I play hockey and basketball too!" Claire added.

Okay, now I knew I was in the wrong house. These people were sports freaks. Suddenly, I suspected a plot. My mom was in on it. She'd sent me here to turn me into an athlete. She wasn't in the hospital at all! She was at home, getting rid of the sofa and the TV and the Wii, replacing them with hard chairs and sporting equipment! She was turning me into a jock so that when we moved to Florida I could say to my dad, "Let's play golf." Yeah, right.

I was awakened from my nightmare by a ball thumping into my chest. "Yeeow!!"

"Pick it up and fire it back!" Claire called.

"I'll fire it back, all right," I muttered under my breath. Then I fired it into the garden pond.

Claire scooped the ball out, drying it on her jeans.

She wandered over to me. "Connor, you've gotta look where you're throwing the ball."

"I did," I retorted.

"No, you didn't," she shot back.

"Did so."

"Did not."

We went on like that for a while until I threw my glove down in disgust. I started to walk away into the house, but Claire looked so hurt that I picked up the glove again.

"Okay, I look where I'm throwing the ball. Like this?" I said, throwing the ball at a garden gnome in the flower bed at her end. Imagine my surprise when I beaned the gnome.

Claire clapped with glee. "That's it, Connor!" She ran to retrieve the ball. Tossing it back she said, "Hit him again!"

I found beaning the gnome to be far more fun than throwing to Claire. She didn't seem to mind. In fact, after a while she just stood to one side and let me bounce balls off his pointy head.

"Try that one, over there," she said, pointing to another gnome at the back fence. I hadn't noticed him before.

"Dopey," Claire remarked.

"Stupid," I replied.

"No," she said. "That's Dopey. That other one is Grumpy." She started pointing out the rest of the gnomes and reciting their names. Suddenly it hit me. They weren't gnomes. They were dwarfs, seven of them.

We spent the next hour lobbing balls at the dwarfs. Claire ran madly around the garden, tossing balls at me from every direction, yelling out dwarf names for me to hit. I was spinning around dizzily.

"Sleepy!"

"Happy!"

"Grumpy!"

I didn't hit them every time, but by the end of the hour, I hit more than I missed.

That's what we were doing when Griffin came home. He came into the yard and watched us for a bit. Then he started to laugh. "My turn!" he shouted.

He joined me in the middle of the lawn, just a few feet away and Claire alternated throwing to us. Finally, we were laughing so hard we all fell into a heap on the grass.

Jane came out to call us in for dinner. "Hi ho, hi ho," she sang. "It's off to eat you go."

9 THE GNOME TEAM

After dinner, Griffin wasted no time messaging his friends to tell them about the dwarf game. The next morning they converged on the Campbells' yard.

Griffin, Claire, and I demonstrated how to play. "Connor invented it," Griffin said.

"Actually, it was Claire's idea," I corrected, as Claire beamed.

Austin, D.J., Matt, and Vincent all clamoured to have a turn. Then Jane came out to see what the commotion was about.

"Hold on," she said. "The garden's taken enough of a beating."

We all groaned our disappointment. "Oh for heaven's sake," Jane responded. "Take the things to the park where you won't do any damage." She went into the house shaking her head.

Griffin yelled, "Everybody grab a dwarf!" With that, he ran to the nearest one and yanked on it. I did the same and was very surprised when it came out of the ground easily. I had thought it would be heavy, but it weighed practically nothing. It was anchored into the ground with a long spike. No wonder the dwarfs hadn't fallen over when I'd beamed them.

Griffin went into the garage and came out with a wagon. We piled a few onto the wagon and carried the rest. As the guys headed off down the driveway, Claire hesitated.

"Claire's got to come too," I said. "She has to call the names." From the way Claire grinned at me, I knew I had made a friend for life.

At the park, we arranged the garden gnomes in a big circle around the pitcher's mound. We met up with some of the other guys and explained what we were doing. We took turns throwing with somebody standing behind the dwarfs to catch the ball while the "pitcher" stood on the mound. After a while, we moved some of the dwarfs farther away until it was really hard to throw the whole distance, at least for me.

We played until lunch time, attracting quite a crowd of spectators. Everybody wanted a chance to play. I could tell that Claire was proud that her game was such a success.

"Hey, Claire, we should open our own theme park," I called to her. She grinned. By the time we finished with the dwarfs, they were a little scuffed up. We pulled up stakes and loaded the wagon. "What are these things made of anyway?" I asked, examining Dopey.

"I dunno," Griffin replied. "Space-age plastic, maybe."

"Where'd they come from?" I asked.

"Outer space, I guess. Isn't that where space-age plastic comes from?" Griffin laughed. "Actually, Grandma gave them to us. My dad hates them, but Mom says we have to put them out for when Grandma comes over."

"What does she do," I asked, "go out and count them?"

"Yep. Once, my dad put them in the garage and Grandma found them and put them all over the front lawn. Dad attacked them with the lawn mower, but Mom made him stop."

"Is that your mom's mom or your dad's mom?" I inquired.

"Dad's," Griffin replied.

Whew! I was beginning to worry that "Grandma" was related to my side of the family.

After that, I started having more fun playing baseball with Griffin and his friends. I think our dwarf drill was actually helping me to react faster. Every day, I could throw the ball farther and more accurately, and Austin stopped calling me "spaghetti arms."

10 NIGHT CRAWLERS

Griffin had been getting increasingly excited about a big Scouts Canada sleepover at the baseball park downtown. By the time the big day arrived, he was practically airborne. We packed a small tent and a few things into the van and headed into town on a sunny Saturday afternoon. It was my first trip to see the Goldeyes with my very own season's ticket.

I'd never before been inside a big sports complex like that. It was kind of like what you see on TV — a whole lot of people eating hot dogs, yelling and waving, and stuff. Griffin was acting like a tour guide, pointing at everything we passed and saying things like, "Guys' bathroom on your right, girls' over there." As if I would need to know where the girls went to the bathroom.

Even though the rest of the Scouts were sitting in a section by themselves, Griffin sat decked out in his Scout uniform with his family. Our seats were pretty good. We were sort of behind home plate, but more on the first base line. From where we sat, I could actually tell whether the pitcher was throwing strikes or balls. At least, I could some of the time. Andrew bought me a program so I could learn about the team.

"You don't need that," said Griffin. "I can tell you anything you need to know about anybody on this team."

"Oh, yeah? What about that guy?" I replied, pointing to the third baseman.

"That's Hit Man," Griffin stated. "Do you know why I call him that?"

"Because he hits the ball a lot?" I guessed.

"Nah, because he gets hit a lot. He's a regular pitch magnet. Sometimes he gets hit more than once in a game."

"What about him?" I asked, pointing to another player.

"I call him Bat Man."

"Okay, I give. Why?"

"'Cause he breaks the most bats of anybody on the team."

We spent the entire game working out names for the players on the team. It wasn't easy. I mean, just because a guy was the pitcher, you couldn't call him Pitch Man. That would be too obvious. Pitch Man was the catcher, who calls the pitches. Besides, there were lots of pitchers, but just one catcher.

By the time the game ended we'd named Walk Man — the guy who drew the most walks, Spider

Man — an outfielder with a pretty amazing ability to climb the fence to rob his opponents of home runs, and my favourite, Garbage Man.

"That name stinks," I said, when Griffin named him.

"Oh yeah?" Griffin said, huffily. "Well what else do you call a guy who bats clean up?"

"What's clean up?" I inquired, not knowing what the term meant.

"That's the guy who cleans the bases when the first three batters get on."

"Huh?" I was confused.

Andrew, overhearing our conversation, explained. "In the batting order, you have your lead-off hitter first. That's someone who's very good at getting on base. Then the next two are also strong hitters. Hopefully, by the time the clean-up hitter comes along, you've got players on base. A clean-up hitter is someone who can bring those players home."

"Oh," I said, brilliantly.

"You'd be a good clean-up hitter, Connor," Andrew added.

"Yeah," Griffin said, "a Garbage Man!"

Claire laughed her head off at that one. And from then on, I was "Garbage Man." Nice, huh?

Once the game ended, I joined Griffin and the Boy Scouts on the field. It looked like there were millions of them marching around the outfield, like ants. Kids were putting tents up everywhere, with barely enough room between them to walk. Everyone was having fun, so I joined in as best I could, considering I knew nothing about Scouting or camping. This sure was turning out to be Connor "Garbage Man" Wells' big summer for new experiences. I wouldn't be short of material for my "What I Did on My Summer Vacation" essay in September.

"Do you want help with the tent?" I asked, as Griffin plopped it out of its bag.

"Nope," he said, and then he flapped his arms around a few times and bingo! There it was — a tent. I had no idea camping was that easy.

"Why don't you check the bag to see what Mom packed us?"

Sitting on top, inside the bag were two pairs of goofy blue-and-red-striped pyjamas.

When Jane had shown them to us earlier in the day, both Griffin and I had groaned.

"Mom! Nobody wears pyjamas like that at a sleepover," Griffin protested.

I didn't say it, but I was pretty sure nobody wore pyjamas like that outside of prison. Maybe not even there.

"You can laugh," said Jane, over his protest, "but you wait. You'll be out there with hundreds of other boys and by wearing these pyjamas you'll be able to find each other instantly."

I didn't care that it made sense. I didn't want striped PJs. Unfortunately, by the time we left, Jane had persuaded Griffin that blue-and-red-striped pyjamas were going to be a hot fashion item among Boy Scouts that weekend.

I rooted around under the PJs. "Fruit," I announced.

"Yuck," Griffin commented. "What else?"

"Toothbrushes."

"Yum. What else?"

I let out a whoop. "Chocolate bars and potato chips! Lots of them. And juice boxes."

"Yay, Mom!"

Austin and D.J. sauntered over. They were sharing a tent in the row behind us.

There was a barbecue with hot dogs and hamburgers. We ate with some kids from another troop who Griffin knew from baseball. A big guy, named Jason, looked me over and said to Griffin, "Is that the guy with the big bat?" Griffin nodded. "I heard about you," Jason said, addressing me.

"Oh, yeah?" I said, cleverly.

"They say you hit a long ball every time."

I had no idea what he was talking about. So I said, "Oh, yeah?" again.

Griffin, my interpreter piped up, "Yeah, he could hit one out of this park, if he wanted to."

Great, I thought. That's the way to do it, Griffin, set me up for a fall.

Jason exchanged glances with his friends. "Betcha he can't," he said.

"Betcha he can," Griffin replied.

"Betcha he won't," somebody said. No wait, that was me.

"What have you got?" Griffin, ignoring me, was still talking to Jason and his crowd. Jason conferred with his guys and they pulled out some baseball cards. They handed these over to Griffin, who looked them over and then passed them to Austin and D.J. I must have become invisible, because they ignored me completely.

Griffin, Austin, and D.J. mumbled among themselves and eventually produced some cards of their own. They turned them over to Jason and the boys, and the ritual was repeated.

"Deal," said Jason.

"Deal," said Griffin.

"No deal," I said, but because I was still invisible, nobody noticed.

"When?" asked Griffin.

"Tonight. Three A.M., at home plate," stated Jason.

"Wait a minute," interrupted Austin. "We don't have a bat."

"I've got a bat," stated Jason.

"How'd you get a bat in here?" Austin demanded. "We're not supposed to have bats."

"That's for me to know and you to find out," replied Jason.

"Wait a minute," I shouted. "Just wait a minute!"

They turned to me. Now that I wasn't invisible

anymore, I continued, "What if I don't want to play?"

Oops, wrong thing to say. Griffin, Austin, and D.J. stared at me in horror. "What?" I said to them. "What did I do wrong?"

My posse took me aside and explained that the honour of the team, the troop, and possibly the known universe was at stake. It was all resting on me.

"Thanks," I said, with all the sarcasm I could muster, but it had no effect. The three of them patted me on the back and returned to Jason to finalize their plan.

After the barbecue, we watched a movie on the giant TV screen. I was the only guy there who wasn't in a Scout uniform. When the movie ended at ten o'clock, we were sent to our tents to turn in. Inside our little tent, we dug out our matching PJs and got changed.

"Now what?" I asked.

Griffin tapped his sports watch. "I set the alarm for three. We meet the rest of the guys then, at home plate."

I don't know if Griffin slept, but I sure didn't. After what seemed like an eternity, I heard the little beep-beep-beep of Griffin's watch. My stomach clenched.

"Let's go," he whispered.

We crawled, cautiously, out of the tent. A nearly full moon illuminated the field and the sea of tents.

"Keep down," Griffin hissed.

We slunk around the edge of the outfield. There were other figures also skulking in the night. Eventually, we all arrived at home plate.

I looked around me and laughed out loud.

"Sshh!" Austin warned.

"Look at us," I hissed. "We look like a chain gang!"

Austin and D.J. were wearing blue-and-red-striped pyjamas just like Griffin's and mine.

Jason eyed us, suspiciously. "What's with the matching outfits? Are you guys some kind of boy band?"

"Everybody in our troop has them," D.J. explained. "It's how we find each other."

So Jane hadn't exactly given us the whole scoop. I don't know whose bright idea that was, considering that all the members of Griffin's Scout troop were decked out in their matching pyjamas, inside their tents.

"Can we get this over with, please?" I pleaded, looking around anxiously.

"Okay," Jason said, getting back to business. "Three strikes, you're out, we win. You don't hit it out of the park, we win. Our guy pitches."

"No," said Griffin. "We alternate. Your guy and me."

"Deal. Who's catching?"

"Me," said D.J.

"Let's go." Griffin gave me a pat on the back and headed for the mound with one of Jason's guys. They didn't actually go all the way to the mound, but paced off the distance that they normally threw from and stopped.

"Can you see them all right?" D.J. asked.

"Yeah," I replied. "How about you?"

"Yeah," he answered. "There's just enough light."

"Just enough light to see," I thought, "and to be seen."

Jason handed me the bat. I stepped up to the plate, nervously. How had I gotten myself into this? Oh yeah, I hadn't. Griffin had done it for me. Some friend. Some cousin!

Griffin trotted in from the "mound," followed by his long moon shadow. "We're going to take a few practice pitches, to warm up," he said.

Once they got that out of the way, Griffin signalled to me. I went back to the plate. My butterflies were mostly gone. I really wanted to get this over with.

The other guy pitched first. His pitch was a little wild. I looked at the rest of the guys behind me. Jason and Austin shook their heads. "Ball," D.J. hissed.

Griffin pitched next. His pitch was good, but I let it go by. If I was going to hit a homer, I didn't want it to be one of Griffin's pitches. I wanted to hit the other guy's pitch. "Strike one," D.J. confirmed, behind me.

Unfortunately, the other guy was still firing balls. There was a little conference going on behind me. I turned around. Finally, Jason waved his guy off. Griffin nodded to me. I nodded back.

Once again, Griffin was on the money, but I whiffed it. Jason's chuckle behind me really fired me up. I turned a menacing glare on him. At least, as menacing a glare as a guy in striped pyjamas can manage in the dark.

It was time to concentrate. Griffin never threw a lot of balls. And I could rely on him to give me something good to hit. "Here goes," I said out loud.

The combination of the moonlight, the city lights, and the dimmed stadium lights around us was just enough to let me see the ball clearly as it came at me. I tensed, then relaxed into my swing. The crack sounded extra loud in the quiet night.

There was only one problem. Nobody could see where the ball went. We all strained our eyes to see beyond the circle of light near home plate. Two things happened.

From the outfield we heard a hollow thud, like the sound of a ball hitting something metallic. Then we were caught in a beam of a very bright light. "What's going on down there?" a voice shouted.

"Run!" We all took off like shots. I dropped the bat and dashed past first base. Once in the forest of tents, I dropped to my knees. I had no idea what our tent looked like.

"Pssst," I heard from my left. "Connor, over here." It was Griffin. I wove my way through tents toward the sound of his voice. A hand shot out and grabbed my leg. I stifled a scream.

Griffin dragged me into our tent. Outside, we could hear the sounds of adult voices. Flashlights bounced off the sides of the tent. I zipped up my sleeping bag, slooowly, forcing my eyes to remain closed. We lay there,

Griffin and I, like corpses, until I drifted off to sleep.

In the morning, Griffin and I kept a low profile. We mingled with the rest of the troop at the pancake breakfast and busied ourselves with packing the tent away. Just as I began to breathe a little easier, I saw one of the leaders heading our way. "Keep your head down, Griffin," I said, under my breath. He glanced up, quickly. "Don't look!" I admonished.

I told myself it was probably nothing. Then the guy approaching us was joined by Griffin's Scout leader and some official-looking guy. This was not good. Griffin and I quickly ducked behind one of the tents that was still up.

Suddenly, the tent collapsed. "Hi, fellas," said Griffin's leader.

"Griffin," he continued, "were you and your cousin playing baseball early this morning?"

"Say no, say no, say no," I said to myself, hoping all the while that Scouts weren't required to tell the truth in addition to helping little old ladies across the street.

Griffin took a long, long time to answer. He looked from me to his leader and back again. I made little tiny head-shaking moves and made my eyes go big. "Yes, sir," he said. "Yes, we were."

Busted! Now I shook my head for real.

"How did you know?" I asked, assuming that Jason had ratted us out.

"Matching pyjamas."

We were being led, like lambs to the slaughter — or in this case, the infield. I didn't ask why and they didn't tell.

"Wait here," said the official-looking guy and he went off toward the dugout.

A few minutes later he emerged from the clubhouse with an older guy in a Goldeyes uniform. He wore wraparound mirrored sunglasses and when he took off his hat, his bald head shone.

I leaned over and whispered to Griffin, "Now we're going to get it."

"Where's Jason and his crew? And Austin and D.J.?" he whispered back.

"I dunno."

The man in the uniform came up to us, smiling. "Hi fellas. I'm the batting coach. Which one of you guys hit the homer last night?"

"Homer?" Griffin brightened. "Hey Connor, we won!"

The batting coach turned to me. "Was that you, Connor?"

"Yeah," I said, embarrassed.

"That's a pretty amazing feat for a Little Leaguer."

"Uh, yeah," I stammered.

"Why don't you boys join us for batting practice?" he said.

"Far out!" Griffin exclaimed.

"That is, right after you apologize to your leader for

breaking the rules." He had a scowl on his face when he said it, but when he turned away from the Scout leaders, he winked at us.

"Oh, yeah," said Griffin. "Sorry."

"Yeah, sorry," I added.

I figured we were getting off easy, but Griffin's troop leader said, "You boys come and see me before you leave today, please." When adults say "please," you know you're in trouble.

I was pretty reluctant to go to batting practice. There were real baseball players hitting balls. And a guy with a camera taking pictures of me! I had a lot of trouble hitting the balls that came out of the machine in the batting cage, until the coach slowed it down. He gave me pointers on how to stand, and how to hold the bat, but mostly he just let me swing away. I hit more than I missed and that felt pretty good.

In the outfield, the last of the Scout tents had been cleared away. Some of the Goldeyes were on the field, stretching and throwing. After the batting machine, they let Griffin pitch to me at home plate and I hit another ball really far. The pitching coach came out to talk to Griffin.

Some of the players started asking me about my team. I was really embarrassed to tell them that I didn't have a team.

"What do you mean you don't have a team?" asked one of them.

I explained a little about why I was in Winnipeg and then I finished by saying, "Hitting's the only thing I can do. Everything else stinks. Bad," I added.

They sure laughed at that.

"Come on, kid," said the guy Griffin called Hit Man. "We know you can hit. Let's try a little running and throwing."

For over an hour, Griffin and I worked out with the team. It was awesome.

I won't say that it changed the way I played baseball, but it sure changed the way people thought I played baseball!

11 TRY, TRY AGAIN

And so I became a minor celebrity among Griffin's and Claire's baseball friends. Except Austin, who was really ticked off that he and D.J. didn't get to play with the big boys.

"How come they just picked you two?" Austin huffed. "We were there too. We had our stripy pyjamas."

"Hey, it's not like they were magic pyjamas, okay?" I said in exasperation. "Besides, where were you when we got that huge lecture on breaking the rules, eh?"

We got reamed out pretty thoroughly over our little escapade by Griffin's Scout leader and the sleepover organizers. We were caught because the security guard saw our faces when everybody else was out of sight. That and the striped pyjamas.

We didn't rat out Austin and D.J., or the others, either. Griffin had to promise never to break the rules again, or he'd be banned from the sleepover next time. The way I saw it, we took the heat for the other guys.

Well, actually Griffin did, because I wasn't a Scout, and who knew what I'd be doing next year?

It was like I said before — I didn't actually play any better right after that morning with the Goldeyes, but everyone thought I did. And because they stopped criticizing me so much, I relaxed and enjoyed myself more. That's when my playing improved.

During our next morning game, I was out playing left field and this time Griffin was batting for the other team. He's a pretty good hitter, as I've said, and he socked one to my side of the field. Fortunately, it was a cloudy day, so I could follow its path through the air. I was playing too far back. I ran to meet it. Ordinarily, I'd be running like mad with my arms flailing around and then the ball would plop down somewhere in front of or behind me. But, not this time. I got right under it, held out my glove, and felt the satisfying slap of leather on leather.

Griffin was out, but they had another guy on first who was barrelling around the bases. There was no time to waste. I unloaded quickly and fired the ball to D.J. It wasn't until after he'd caught it and tagged the runner out that I realized how far I'd thrown. Not only was it farther than I'd ever thrown successfully, but I didn't draw D.J. off the bag. That was the first time I'd thrown for distance and accuracy. It felt good.

You'd have thought I was a Golden Glove candidate, the way Griffin raved. That is, he raved about my catch after he complained about my catching him out.

"You know, cousin," he said, "you should cut me some slack. If you want to be a star, why don't you throw Austin out?"

"I don't have to," I laughed. "He never hits the ball!"

"Hey," Austin grumbled, "I hit sometimes."

"Oh yeah?" said D.J. "When?"

"Last week," replied Austin. "I hit the catcher with the bat."

That's what I liked about Austin. He could laugh at himself.

Austin may not have hit much, but he was a fairly good defensive player, which was, I was quickly learning, very important to the team.

A few days later, Andrew pulled some strings and got me another chance to show the Spinners how I was doing. I was pretty nervous about that, but the whole family got behind me and we practised like mad.

With my second try out looming, I started to get anxious all over again. I was beginning to think my fluke homer was just setting me up for another disaster.

When I called my mom that night, I decided not to tell her about the tryout the next day. She was already out of the hospital and staying with my grandparents in Millgrove, north of Burlington. Sometimes she sounded a bit groggy and sometimes she would tell me the same thing twice, or she wouldn't remember what I'd told her the night before. It was creepy.

She kept saying she was okay and getting better all the time, but she sure didn't sound like it.

What scared me the most was that she didn't joke with me anymore. I'd say something that, in the past, she would have had a great comeback for, but not now. Our conversations were pretty one-sided. I'd tell her what I was doing and she'd say, "That's great, Connor" or "I'm so glad you're having fun." It always sounded like she was falling asleep.

All the way to the practice the next evening, Andrew and Griffin kept building me up, telling me what I was doing well and to relax and stuff. They were really encouraging, and by the time we got there, I felt pretty good. Andrew went to talk to the coaches while Griffin and I hung out with the team.

When Andrew came back, he said, "Connor, you can join the kids on the field." I was so relieved that I wouldn't have the coaches breathing down my neck. I grabbed a glove and trotted out with Griffin.

I'd seen enough of Griffin's practices to know the drills. For an hour and a half I batted, ran, threw, and caught. I must have done it well enough because, when it ended, Coach Gelber waved me over.

"You're looking a lot better, Connor," he said. "You can tell Andrew and Griffin that you're going to play with us."

"Really?"

"You're on the team. Pick up your jersey next time."

Coach Gelber gave me a quick smile and sauntered off.

I ran over to where Griffin was sitting with Austin and D.J. "I'm in!" I shouted. "I'm on the team!" The three of them jumped up and high-fived me and each other in jubilation.

Just to be sure I wasn't mistaken, I asked Andrew to go check with Coach Gelber. When he came back, he was smiling a great big smile. "Connor's definitely going to play with you guys," he said to Griffin. To me he said, "Connor, you've done well. We're proud of you."

I felt my face redden. I wasn't used to all that gushy stuff. Fortunately, Griffin and D.J. punched my shoulders and told me I still had a lot to learn. That felt more like it.

Mom was pretty excited for me when I called her. She told me that my dad had called her from Florida. She said that the next time he called, she was going to give him my telephone number in Winnipeg. I thought it was a good sign that he'd called. Maybe he was ready to have us join him in Orlando. "Did you tell him about my homer?" I asked.

"No, Connor," Mom replied. "I forgot."

"Maybe you could call him back," I suggested. "Maybe I could call him."

"No, I don't think so, honey," she said, the tiredness creeping into her voice again. I let it drop.

As always, after I finished talking to Mom, Jane got on the phone with her. I never learned anything more from listening to Jane's side of the conversations. That night was no different.

When Griffin and I turned in, we talked for a long time about the team and what fun it was going to be to have me play with them. He told me all about the different teams they played against. By the time I drifted off to sleep, he'd given me a rundown of all the pitchers and hitters in his league. It was a lot to think about.

★ ★ ★

I woke up out of a deep sleep. It felt like I'd been asleep for a long time, but a glance at Griffin's alarm clock told me that it was less than an hour. I had to go to the bathroom.

A light from Jane and Andrew's room lit up the hall. I could hear them talking as I passed by. The television was playing in the background. I was almost to the bathroom when I heard Jane say my mom's name. That stopped me in my tracks. I crept back quietly and stood with my ear to the door.

"He should have known better than to call and tell her that," Jane said. "He knows full well how sick she is."

Andrew murmured something I couldn't make out. Jane went on, her voice rising in volume a bit. "I think it's cruel. Imagine calling your ex-wife and telling her you just had a baby with your new wife." On hearing that, I breathed a sigh of relief. They weren't talking about Mom after all. My parents weren't divorced. My dad didn't have a new wife. I turned to go back down the hall toward the bathroom again.

"How is she going to tell Connor he's got a half brother? She hasn't even told him they're divorced."

I stopped dead. My heart skipped a beat as I broke into a cold sweat. I didn't want to hear more but my feet wouldn't carry me away.

Jane's voice was angry. "What was he thinking, calling her now? For heaven's sake, she's got cancer!"

Stumbling into the bathroom, I clamped my hands over my ears. I collapsed onto the floor, shaking in the dark.

12 DECEIVED

I don't know how long I was in the bathroom. When I crept back to bed, I didn't look at the clock. I lay awake for a long time, with my head spinning. It was too much to think about and in my mind, I jumped back and forth between fear for my mom and anger at my dad. When I finally fell asleep, my dreams were a jumble of images, with me shouting at both my parents. When I finally awoke, I didn't feel any better. I was tired and angry.

I skulked down to breakfast and poured myself a bowl of cereal and milk. Griffin was already eating. He looked at me and said, "Don't worry, Connor. It's going to be fine. You wait."

I almost dropped my spoon. "What do you know about it?" I sputtered, wondering how he had found out. Maybe Jane had seen me listening outside her bedroom door.

"Well, I don't know, exactly," Griffin explained, "but if I were you, I'd be nervous too. I was nervous the first time I pitched a game."

Relieved, I looked up at him. He thought I was nervous about the game that night. "Yeah, well, thanks," I mumbled. "I'll be okay."

"We'll just practise lots today and you'll be ready," he said.

I couldn't say I was in the mood for baseball that day, but I couldn't very well back out. What would I tell the team?

Austin took charge of me the minute we arrived at the park. He'd appointed himself my coach, taking me off to practise, throwing and fielding grounders. His constant chatter started driving me crazy. Finally I told him I needed to hit the ball for a while. I could see he was a little hurt by the gruff way I'd spoken, but he didn't say anything. The other guys were having batting practice, with Griffin pitching to them.

I nabbed a bat and took a place in line. Austin headed out to field the hits, casting me a quizzical look as he went. I looked away.

The first pitch that Griffin threw, I imagined the ball was my dad's head. Yeah, I know that was pretty nasty, but I was mad. I hit it hard enough to knock the cover off and lined it so far foul of first base that Austin yelled "Fore" to some kids playing in the sand pit. Fortunately, the ball missed them, because I don't think they had a clue what Austin meant.

After that, I lost the magic and couldn't hit anything. On the way home, Griffin asked me if I was okay.

"Yeah," I said, "I'm fine."

"Well you didn't look it," he replied. "Your shoulders were way up around your ears. That's probably why you were fouling off so much."

"It was just a practice," I said, in my defence. "I'll do better in the game."

* * *

We went out for hamburgers before the game, meeting Austin and his family at the restaurant. Austin and Griffin kept talking about how we were going to cream the competition that night. They were working out how many at-bats we'd each get and how many homers I could hit. I said nothing, just ate my burger and kept my head down.

When we arrived at the ballpark, Coach Gelber handed me my uniform jersey. Andrew surprised me with new shoes. I was ready. At least that's what they thought. When Coach Gelber had said I'd be playing some innings, I hadn't expected to be starting the game. We were the visiting team, which meant that unless the first three guys went down, I'd probably have an at-bat in the first inning.

"Don't worry about their pitcher," Griffin advised.

"Yeah," Austin added, "even I can hit him."

D.J. and the rest of the kids on the bench laughed. D.J. led off with a nice hit that put him on first. The next kid flied out, then Austin struck out.

"He's just havin' a good night," he said, as he walked by me on deck.

Coach Markovic gave me a thumbs-up as I took my place at home plate. Remembering what Griffin had said about my shoulders, I shook them a couple of times to loosen up. I wasn't ready for the first pitch. It zipped by and I knew it was a strike before the umpire called it.

I didn't have to look at our bench to feel the intensity of my teammates' looks. The pitcher went into his windup and I drew a breath. I must have blinked because my swing was late. The ball was in the catcher's glove and it was strike two.

"Settle down," I told myself. "You can do this." I should have told myself not to talk to myself when I was batting because that little conversation bought me another strike and the long walk back to the bench.

Most of the guys were already on their way onto the field when I retrieved my glove. I was glad not to have to face them after my poor performance.

I took up my usual spot in left field, beyond D.J. Thankfully, Griffin was having an even better day than the other pitcher. He faced three batters. Two struck out, the other grounded to second.

Griffin was up first, for us. He sure was hot that night. He smacked a beauty into deep centre and made it to third. I was jealous. That should have been me, hitting long balls. In the stands, I could hear Jane, Andrew, and Claire cheering their heads off.

Vincent hit cleanly past first base and brought Griffin home to loud applause. Griffin sat down beside me, grinning his fool head off. "Nice hit," I said, trying to be generous.

"Thanks," he replied. "We're on a roll tonight."

"Yeah," I said, lamely. "On a roll."

With Vincent on first, the next batter walked and Vincent advanced to second. They stayed there while the next two batters struck out. We were back to the top of the order. D.J. hit one over the head of the third baseman, but the left fielder was on it like lightning. He lobbed the ball to third and put the runner out.

Back to work. I had high hopes that Griffin would save me from any fielding duties, but before that thought even left my head, a ball was on its way to me. It bounced just a metre from where I stood. I felt it hit my glove and started running toward second hoping to cut the distance I'd have to throw. The runner was around first. I reached into my glove. The ball was gone. Confused, I looked around me. I was dimly aware of voices calling my name. D.J., Griffin, and Austin were all pointing at something behind me.

The ball was on the grass a short distance behind me. D.J. was running in my direction. I waved him off and grabbed the ball. In my haste to throw, the ball squirted out of my hand and wound up in just about the same place I'd found it.

The runner was now heading for third, so D.J. ran

back to defend his position. I was paralysed. The ball was still on the ground when the runner passed third on his way home. I'd managed to turn his single into a home run. Tie game, thanks to me.

At that moment, I wanted to stay in left field forever, rather than face my teammates. Fortunately, they were kept busy putting away the next three batters. When the time came, I skulked to the bench.

Griffin, as always, was Mr. Positive. "Don't worry about it," he said. "I shouldn't have given him anything to hit."

"Yeah," I thought. "Like it was his fault. I don't think so." "I was sure I had it," I said, explaining. "Then I just lost it, completely."

There were two batters ahead of me, then I would have a chance to redeem myself.

They walked our first two batters. That brought me to the plate with two men on and nobody out. An ideal situation.

"He's throwing garbage," Griffin said. "Just keep your eye on the ball."

"I will," I replied, feeling a little more confident.

I decided to go back to world-saving strategy, but try as I might, I kept getting sidetracked. I started out imagining the pitches were hand grenades, but by the time they crossed the plate, they were Dads or little brothers. I knew this was wrong and it was getting me worked up. Besides, I'd lost track of the count.

Too embarrassed to ask, I swore to myself that I would tattoo the next pitch. Trouble was, the next pitch was practically around my ankles and I swung anyway. Somehow I connected with the ball, but it only drooled out toward third. The catcher was on it in a flash and within seconds they'd tagged the runners out at third and second. I limped to first. Two down, slow man on first.

I was hoping that Griffin would save me but he popped up and we were out of it. I trotted in to get my mitt, but Coach Gelber waved me over.

"I'm going to send Mitch into left, Connor," he said. "You can take a rest."

I hung my head. Two innings and my Little League career was over. I barely watched the rest of the inning. When the team came in to bat, I avoided Griffin's eyes the whole time.

When it was over they all tried to cheer me up.

"Don't worry," Griffin said. "You had a bad day, but we won anyway!" But when he cast a worried glance at the coaches, I knew what Griffin really thought. I'd blown it.

13 SHOWDOWN

On the way home in the van, everyone was so encouraging it was disgusting. I sat there, beside Griffin, silently steaming, and wondering if they all knew the truth about my family. What if they'd known all along and that was why they were being so nice to me? They probably thought I was a loser kid from some movie-of-the-week type of broken home.

I wanted to know the truth. I decided to ask when we passed the red-slide park. Then, I figured I would say something when we passed the fake dog. But I was so angry that I thought it would be better to ask when we got into the house. My heart was pumping loudly as I followed Jane into her office.

"Connor," she said, "shall we call your mom? You know, your calls are the high point of her day. She told me that yesterday."

"Aha," I thought, "and what else did she tell you?" Before I could answer her, Jane was dialling.

I snatched the phone out of her hand, ignoring the

surprised look on her face. "Hi, Granma," I said, sharply. "Can I talk to Mom?" Behind me, Jane left the room and closed the door.

"Hi, honey," Mom said, in that weak voice she had at the end of the day. "How was the baseball game?"

"Great," I said. "Just great. We won."

"Oh, that's wonderful, Connor. I'm so glad you're having fun." She said that every day. Well, I wasn't having fun today.

"How about you?" I asked, sarcastically. "Are you having fun?"

She laughed a little. "Oh yeah, I'm having the time of my life. I'm just fine."

This small talk was making me crazy. "How's Dad?" I threw in, for spite.

"I'm sure he's fine," she said, wearily.

"You're fine, he's fine, I'm fine, everybody's fine. Fine, fine, fine, it's a fine day and I'm having a fine time." My shouting started a stampede in the hallway. I waited for the door to open, but nobody came in.

"Connor? Connor! What's wrong?"

"What!" I shouted into the phone, aware of the alarm in her voice.

"What's going on?" she asked.

"What's going on?" I said, my voice rising. "You're asking *me* what's going on?"

I didn't give her a chance to answer. "I know what's going on. I know about Dad and his baby and your divorce and, you know what else? I know you have cancer. THAT'S WHAT'S GOING ON!"

"Oh my God, oh my God," Mom cried. "How do you know? Who told you?"

My heart was still beating like mad and sweat was pouring off me. I felt light-headed, almost faint. "It doesn't matter who told me, Mom. *You* should have told me. You!" I shouted. "Why did you lie to me?" I asked, bitterly.

She was silent for a long time. I waited, letting my heart calm down. I could hear her crying on the phone.

"I'm so sorry, Connor. I should have told you everything, but I was afraid of hurting you. We were doing all right without your dad. I kept waiting for the right moment to tell you that he wasn't coming back, but it never came. I guess I chickened out."

I snorted a little half-chuckle. She sounded so sorry.

"You got a divorce and everything and you never told me," I said, quietly now. "And now he's got another son."

"Yes," she said, "your brother."

"Half-brother," I reminded her. "I don't want to see him. I don't want half a brother."

"Don't say that, Connor," she said. "I'm sorry."

"I know. You already said that," I replied.

"No, I mean about not trusting you with the truth about my cancer. I didn't think you could handle something like that."

"You'd better tell me now, Mom," I said. "I can handle it."

"It's called lymphoma. I won't bore you with the details, honey. It's serious, but they caught it early and with chemotherapy, the doctors think my prognosis is good. Do you know what that means, 'prognosis'?"

"Not really," I admitted.

"It means that my outlook for the future is good. Our future is good."

"Did you have an operation?"

"No, just chemotherapy. It makes me sick to my stomach. And I'm more tired than I've been in my whole life. There are other symptoms, but those are the worst."

She went on to explain it all in detail. By the time we hung up, I felt both good and sad. I felt good that I knew everything and that was a real weight off my back. But at the same time, I was really sad about Dad and Mom and me. I shouldn't have been so mad at my mom for not telling me about the divorce and stuff. I mean, Dad could have told me himself.

Late that night, I sat in front of Griffin's computer in the dark, slowly typing out a letter to my dad. In it, I told him exactly what I thought of him and his new family. I told him what a rotten dad I thought he was and how sorry I felt for his new kid to have such a rotten dad. You could say I was mad.

When I finished, I printed it out and took it to the

bathroom to read. It was long — six pages. I read it through three times. Then I ripped it into little pieces and flushed it down the toilet.

★ ★ ★

The next day, everybody treated me differently. It was like I was sick or someone had died, the way they were so polite and extra kind. It made me uncomfortable. I was tired and I just wanted to lie around and watch TV.

Jane came into the family room where I was sitting alone. "I talked to your mom this morning," she started. "I'm glad you know everything, Connor. I wanted to tell you but . . . well, I couldn't."

"Yeah, that's okay," I said, avoiding her eyes.

"Did you overhear me talking to Andrew the other night?" she asked.

"Yeah," I said.

"I thought I heard someone in the hallway. I'm sorry. That was certainly not the way you should have heard about it. Will you forgive me, Connor?"

"Yeah," I said. She looked at me a bit longer and then left me alone.

Claire came roaring into the family room and threw my baseball glove into my lap.

"Hey!" I yelled.

"Hey, yourself," she replied. "Stop moping around. You stunk yesterday. You need practice. Let's go!"

I was going to protest, but she grabbed my hand and before long I was hard at work beaning dwarfs.

Later that evening, we went to another Goldeyes game. We went early so Griffin, Claire, and I could watch the team warming up. While Andrew and Jane waited in line at the concession stands, the three of us went down to the edge of the field to get a better look.

The batting coach walked by and said hello. "How're you boys doing?" he asked. "How's the hitting, young fella?" he said to me.

"It's okay, I guess," I mumbled.

"He's in a slump," Claire announced.

"Well, you keep at it," the coach said to me. "That's the only way to get better. Practise. Never give up."

"Thanks," I said.

"I told 'ya," Claire said, punching me on the arm. "I could be a coach."

"You already are," I laughed. "You're the dwarf coach."

"Never give up," he'd said. I'd tried everything else. Why not that?

14 HOT BAT

While I struggled not to give up on myself, Coach Claire had decided not to give up on me either. She had me running, throwing, and catching practically every waking hour. Even when I was in the park, playing with Griffin and the boys, Claire hung out on the sidelines, giving me pointers.

I don't know where that kid got her information, but it sure helped me out. As the days went by, I actually got better. And believe it or not, I hit the ball even farther than before.

At every one of the Spinners games, after my disastrous first outing, I'd sat out most of the games on the bench. It was hard, but I enjoyed being with the team. I'd had a few uneventful innings in the outfield and a couple of homers at the plate, but it wasn't enough to convince the coaches that I should start the games.

One game, I was still on the bench at the top of the last inning. I didn't know how the standings worked, but it was obvious that this was a game we needed to win. Our team was up to bat. We were down by two runs and our bats had been running cold. Worse, Griffin was struggling with his control.

D.J., always reliable, hit a dribbler to the shortstop and reached first. The next batter struck out and the one after that walked. Two on, one out. Not bad odds. Then Vincent popped up and it was two out. Austin was on deck. Beside me, Griffin groaned. The rest of the bench groaned in agreement. Austin was not the clutch hitter we needed in this situation.

Then Austin was heading back to the bench and Coach Gelber was shouting "substitution" and waving and pointing at me.

"Me?" I said, pointing to myself. Coach Gelber nodded.

Surprised, I jumped up. Jamming on a batting helmet, I strode up to the plate and took a couple of practice swings.

From behind his mask, their catcher said, "It's Mr. Long Ball." I turned around, peering into the mask. "Jason," I said, recognizing the kid from the Scout sleepover.

"It was foul," he said. I knew he was referring to my hit at CanWest Global Park.

"It was not," I said, as the first pitch came low and outside.

"Ball one," said the umpire.

"It bounced foul," said Jason.

"It did not," I said, letting an ankle-biter go by.

"Ball two," announced the umpire.

Their pitcher was tiring. A walk would be as good as a base hit, I thought. But it wouldn't score a run. I needed this guy to give me something to hit.

"They found it in the seats on the first-base side," Jason hissed.

The ball was on its way to me, belt high, at good speed. "They did NOT!" I exclaimed, swinging away with all my might.

No doubt about that ball. It was long gone. I watched the centre fielder leap vainly for it. And then I strutted around the bases to the cheers of my team-mates. Now that felt good! I stole a glance at Coach Gelber. He was all smiles.

The next batter flied out and the boys grabbed their gloves to go out and take their last stand. I was uncertain what to do. Coach Gelber waved me onto the field, hollering, "You stay in the game, Connor. Centre field."

That was Austin's territory. I'd never played centre before. It was busier than left and that's why Austin played it. He was a good fielder. I, on the other hand, was a notoriously bad fielder. And there I was, with my team up by one run and with a struggling pitcher. Oh man, it was all resting on me.

I looked around to check my wingmen. Then I realized that the distance from centre field to the infield was a lot greater. Yipes!

Fortunately, the first batter struck out. Good thing Griffin still had some juice. The second batter got on when a grounder got past our first baseman. He stole second base moments later. Not good. No double play. No easy way out. And then a looper to shallow right put men on third and first.

Griffin got the next batter to pop up, but before the applause died, he walked the next guy to load the bases. One out away from a win, one hit away from disaster. I knew just how Griffin felt.

And up came Jason. He was a long way away, but I could feel the heat of his sneer from centre field. Vincent waved me farther back.

Griffin's pitch was a carbon copy of the one I had hit. Jason whacked it hard, straight to centre field and straight at me. I was momentarily paralysed, and when I recovered my senses it was too late to run back. That ball was coming at me, way over my head.

Suddenly, I found springs in my legs. I leaped high in the air, with my glove stretched far over my shoulder. Miraculously, the ball hit leather. I slammed the door on it. Horrified, I watched it squirt out as I tumbled backwards. I was falling onto my back. The ball was falling with me. I hit the turf with an "oomp" that nearly knocked the wind out of me. My arm jerked up reflexively. The ball was still in the air.

I was a leather magnet. I plucked that ball right out of the air, with my bare hand.

And there I lay, waving the ball in my hand, until my teammates arrived, cheering, and piled on.

15 GOLDEN

My baseball summer flew by too fast. Between pick-up games, practices, real games, and Goldeyes games, I'd had a lifetime of baseball action. It wasn't the summer I'd imagined for myself. It was better.

After our big blowout, Mom and I were able to talk about everything that was happening with her treatment. By the end of August, she was midway through her chemotherapy. I was going to have to stay with her at Granma and Grandpa's for the first two months of school. Just before I had to go home, she told me she had some news.

"Don't you laugh at me, Connor," she warned, "but I'm as bald as a billiard ball."

Of course I laughed. I tried to imagine my mother without her curly blond hair.

"And what's worse," she went on, "I have a strange ridge right on top of my head. Your grandfather calls it 'Rattlesnake Point.'" Rattlesnake Point is a conservation area north of Burlington.

I felt my own head, but I couldn't feel anything. "Are you getting a wig?" I asked.

"No, I think I'll just wait until my hair grows back. Maybe you could loan me your Spinners cap. Besides, I don't mind being bald. It's very cool."

I thought it was cool too, although I don't think that's what she meant by "cool."

I only had one more game to play with the team before I had to go home. I got to play the whole game, back in left field. By the end, I realized how much I'd enjoyed learning to play baseball. I was pretty good, and there was nobody on the team who could hit as well as me. I was proud of that.

"You're coming back next year, right, Connor?" Austin asked.

"I dunno," I replied.

"I think you should," Griffin agreed. "We need you. You're our power hitter."

"Thanks," I said, embarrassed by the attention. "You guys have to come to Burlington. Any time. We can go to the Rogers Centre." I could just imagine what my mom would say if the whole team showed up at our door.

We won the game, and I'm proud to say that it was thanks to me and a couple of beauty homers. As I came in from the field, the team converged on me and piled on me again, even though I'd had an uneventful last inning.

Just at the point when I thought I'd be crushed to death, they rolled off and Griffin pulled me to my feet. Everybody turned to look at Austin, who was holding something behind his back.

Austin, grinning like mad, pulled his arm around and poked me in the stomach with a bat. "It's for you," he said.

The bat was painted shiny gold. It had writing all over it. I looked closer. Everybody had signed the bat. "Turn it over, Connor," Griffin said.

I rolled the bat around in my hands. It was engraved: "Connor Wells — Power Hitter." There was a little Spinners logo underneath. It was my first baseball trophy. I didn't know what to say, so I just smiled.

★ ★ ★

"Christmas break, you promised," I reminded Jane. She and Andrew had agreed to send Griffin to Burlington for a visit during the holidays.

"I know," she said, folding clean T-shirts and shorts for me to pack into my old hockey bag. "He'll be there. As long as your mother's up to it."

"She's going to be okay," I said confidently. "She just has to wear her Spinners cap for a while."

Griffin and Claire were sitting glumly on the floor, watching as Jane helped me pack. "It's not going to be the same around here," Griffin moped.

"Yeah," Claire agreed, "Connor's a way better brother than Griffin."

I laughed. "Thanks, Coach. You're a pretty excellent brother yourself."

I made Jane promise me something else too. Before I left, we took a little trip to the mall, just the two of us. I wanted to get something for my mom. At first I had a hard time deciding what to get her. Then, we passed a store and I saw just what I wanted.

An hour later, I emerged from the store — bald as a billiard ball. I was ready to go home to Burlington and my mom.

It was my second trip on an airplane, and I knew exactly what to expect.

CHECK OUT THESE OTHER TITLES FROM LORIMER'S SPORTS STORIES SERIES:

Curve Ball
by John Danakas

Tom Poulos is looking forward to a summer of baseball. But instead of playing catcher for the Jarvis Badgers, Tom finds himself on a plane to Winnipeg, where he'll spend the summer with an uncle he doesn't even know.

"Fun and immensely enjoyable. . . Ball fans will enjoy this book."

— Ken Setterington. Quill & Quire

Double Play
by Sara Cassidy

Allie's invited to play on the boy's baseball team but then her step-brother announces he wants to play on the girl's team!

Commended — A Junior Library Guild Selection – 2013
*Commended — Best Books for Kids & Teens *Starred Selection* – Canadian Children's Book Centre – 2013*

LORIMER

Hoop Magic
by Eric Howling

Orlando really wants to be a star player, but despite his best efforts he can't quite seem to make the right play at the right time. His biggest contributions to the team are his ability to get them energized and to call the shots. But accepting these as his special talents means he has to give up his dream of playing basketball.

"Hoop Magic is an exciting story about basketball and adversity. . .This book would be an excellent class novel for individual reading or as a read-aloud choice." Highly Recommended.
— Deborah Mervold CM:
Canadian Review of Materials

Game Face
by Sylvia Gunnery

Basketball player Jay has to focus on what's weak and make it strong.

Commended — Best Books for Kids & Teens – Canadian Children's Book Centre – 2013

Replay
by Steven Sandor

Warren's dreams of being a football star are in reach — but does he have to cheat to win?

"Sandor's experiences as a sportswriter and broadcaster are evident, creating an authentic basis for the story line. He effectively weaves strong life lessons about winning, losing, and fair play into Warren's story in a manner that is subtle and highly engaging."

— Booklist

1884